A BOOK OF FIELDS

A BOOK OF FIELDS

Stephen Billias

Odeon Press

Printed in the United States of America

ISBN 978-1-7335750-0-3

Published by Odeon Press
www.Odeonpress.com

And of everything earthly there remained
Only your daily bread,
A fellow man's kind word,
And the pure voice of the field.

Anna Akhmatova from
The Echoing Green anthology

For Bela and Sophia

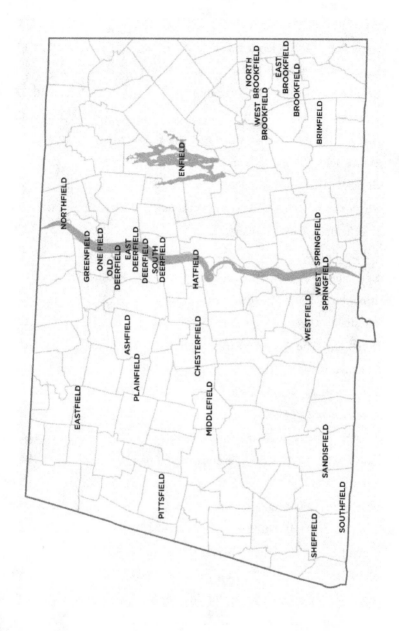

Preface

"*A writer must have an address*" Isaac Bashevis Singer declared. My address is the Pioneer Valley of Western Massachusetts, and more particularly for this book, those valley and hill towns ending in "field": Ashfield, Deerfield, Greenfield and so forth. Twenty-five towns, twenty-four of them real, one imaginary, and one field that is not a town. I have lived or spent time in all of them, especially the imaginary one. The Pioneer Valley (and slightly beyond) is a magical land, populated not by magicians or wizards but by very real human beings. Taken together, the stories in *A Book of Fields* are a portrait of a world that is rapidly disappearing. The lush farms and fields of the Connecticut River basin are shrinking every year. The agricultural way of life is giving way to suburbia. The people change as the land use changes. This book is about these towns, and the men and women who inhabit them: hardy, independent, passionate, hardheaded, sometimes a little crazy.

Each story has character types and locales that will be recognizable to anyone who has spent any time in the area. A few of the stories share characters. Some of the stories contain a crime, or something like one, but this is not a crime novel. It's a deceptively simple book about the people of the Pioneer Valley.

Greenfield: A Robbery at Wade's Diner

Every morning I ate at Wade's Diner, in the center of Greenfield, right off the town square. It was the closest thing we had to a Jeffersonian democracy, or was it a Chautauqua camp gathering? Practically anybody of note in town was at Wade's for breakfast. The mayor, Stanley Bisquette, wearing his trademark bow tie and a starched shirt every day, his grey hair slicked straight back, his pants pressed to frightening crispness. John Paslowski, the police chief, his belly bulging out of his uniform in unsightly places, his grey hair in a brush cut, his square jaw working at a plate of heavy breakfast food. And various harmless ne'er-do-wells, idlers and gabblers who had nothing better to do every morning than come to Wade's Diner. Every day we solved the world's problems and went home with our bellies full, and the next day we came back and ran through them again.

Wade Letourneau, the owner of Wade's Diner, was a Vietnam vet, with a Semper Fi tattoo on his right shoulder that he displayed prominently by wearing flannel shirts with the sleeves cut off. He'd been a cook in the Marines, and had served a battalion of up to 800 at a time. Making a few omelets on a morning was child's play to him. He was nobody's fool. He was the voice of the town. He'd owned a bar called The Caboose out by the rail yard in Deerfield until there'd been some trouble and he moved into town and started the diner. Well, that's not exactly right. He took over the diner, which had begun to molder, and brought it back to a naval spit and polish state. Pretty soon it was the scuttlebutt, the water cooler, the place where much of the town's business was transacted. The place where we gathered to share news and gossip.

So here were Al and Jim, buddies who lived together on a pig farm outside of town because their wives had left them. They were arguing over how the Army press secretary was talking about a recent 'collateral damage' episode in Afghanistan, or was it Syria or Iraq?

"Of course they said it wasn't them," said Jim. "It's never them. Of course they used the lowest number for the casualty total, and who knows what the real number was, but you know it's more than what they said, Al. You know it is."

"Why do you say that, Jim?"

"Because it's always that way, Al. Did you ever hear them say '*Oh, we killed many more innocent civilians than that?*'"!

"No."

"No. It's always '*It wasn't our fault. The numbers are inflated. The enemy did it to themselves.*' Or some other such crap."

And then later here's our mayor Bisquette, who looks like he should be more in control than he is, trying to explain to chief Paslowski why the school budget was going up:

"We had to fix the middle school roof. That exasperated it."

"Huh?

"That exasperated the situation."

"Oh. Yeah." Mutual misunderstanding, and yet they understood each other perfectly.

"You have to address the undeveloped dependencies," the mayor continued.

"Undeveloped dependencies? You mean like my nephew Bob who lives in our in-law and never has a job? He's an undeveloped dependency."

"I'm talking more in a technological sort of way, Chief."

So, there we were, the good people of Greenfield, having breakfast just like every other day, reading the *Greenfield Recorder*, sopping up our greasy eggs with white bread toast, regaling each other with lies and fish tales and petty arguments. Three men walked into the diner. They had ski masks on.

"Everybody hands on the tables, this is a robbery!" the first man in shouted. He was nervous, twitchy. Strands of long blond hair escaped from under the mask. He might have had dreadlocks, I couldn't tell. He was holding a large gun, probably a semi-automatic pistol, though I'm no expert on these things.

"Get the f#%k out of here," Wade said.

"Shut up, man, or I'll smash your ugly face. Open the cash drawer."

"Won't," Wade said.

Police chief Paslowski swiveled on his stool and stared at the three robbers. He spoke quietly to Wade.

"Wade, do as the boy says."

"Won't, John. Tell 'em how far we are from the police station."

"Quarter mile."

"Tell 'em how far they'll get after they leave my place and you call it in."

"'Bout the same."

"Why don't you stop this nonsense and sit down for breakfast? How do you boys like your eggs?" Wade asked.

The second and third robbers fidgeted and looked to the first one who was obviously the ringleader.

"We're not here for f#%kin' eggs, we're here for money! Now open that cash drawer."

"Won't."

I wasn't going to be a hero. I wanted to make sure I could get out the door if shooting started, so I started edging that way. The second robber, a heavyset young man who was having trouble breathing under his ski mask, waved his gun at me.

"Stop." I stopped. "Back." I backed up. The third robber, a scrawny kid who didn't look old enough to drink or vote, snorted a laugh. He liked seeing his elders bossed around at the point of a gun.

"Make 'im walk on all fours an' grunt like a pig."

"Shut up!" said the blond one. As he spoke I recognized his voice. It was Emmet, my neighbor Carl

Vincent's son. I realized at once that I'd better not let Emmet know I recognized him. Witnesses get shot for that. But now that I knew who he was, I took a closer look at the other two, and I thought I could name them both. I was pretty sure it was the brothers Jesse and Anthony Smolenski, a couple more town kids, sons of Bob Smolenski, the town barber. (Okay, there were three barber shops on town, but everybody in Wade's Diner went to Bob's.) I had a feeling there were other people in the diner who could have said who they were also. How stupid, to rob a place where *'everybody knows your name'*. I suppose you don't tend to make good decisions when you're hopped up on meth, or whatever drug habit it was they were stealing money to feed. But dammit, former Marine Wade wasn't going to let them have his hard-earned cash without a fight, and we might all get shot as a result.

"Stop f$#kin' around. Get their wallets," the blond ringleader said. For a second nobody moved. We (the diners) outnumbered the robbers by about four to one, and I suspected that besides Chief Paslowski several other men in the place had firearms on them. The Chief put up his right hand and reached across with his left hand to drop his gun belt, and then slowly reached into his back pocket and pulled out a fat wallet. *Jesus, he must get back pains from sitting on that thing all day*, I thought nonsensically, as the rest of us (except Wade) mechanically did the same.

"Gimme a to-go bag there Chuck."

"My name's not Chuck."

"Sure it is. Every hash-slinger is named Chuck."

"F$#k ya, get it yourself," said Wade.

"Move outta the way." Wade moved. He respected the gun, if not the person holding it. I saw Wade's right hand clench and relax. He wanted to throw a punch so bad as the blond robber inched past him, never turning his back, but he held off because he didn't want others to get hurt. At least that's what he told us later, after it was over. It could have turned into a bloodbath at any second. I had to do something. Like I said, I'm no hero. I'm afraid of guns, unlike most of the men in the diner at that moment. But I stepped between them and faced Emmet and said:

"We'll give you the money but you have to promise me one thing."

Emmet gave me a wicked stare. "What's that?"

"You'll come back to Wade's Diner sometime after they let you out and have breakfast with us."

Emmet laughed. Jesse and Anthony laughed. Everybody in the diner laughed. They knew we knew who they were, and we knew they knew. And we knew they knew they were all going to jail, and go to jail they did. They grabbed the money from the wallets everyone offered them, and ran out. Twenty minutes later Emmet crashed their getaway car into a granite boundary marker off Colrain Road. Chief John showed up with half the guys from Wade's Diner including me trailing him. The first local patrolman had already arrived and put the three of them against their overturned Dodge.

"Jesus Christ, Emmet. You're a better young man than this. Go dry out in that jail for a while. You two also—straighten up!" He spoke without looking at Jesse and Anthony. "I'm so disgusted I'm thinking about changing barbers." He turned away, and the three would-be robbers were led away, none of them injured any more than bloody scratches despite the violent rollover.

We talked about it every day for about three weeks, then maybe every other day, then once a week, then it just became something that had happened in Wade's Diner on Main Street in Greenfield, once upon a time. The boys went to jail. They were back at Wade's Diner as customers almost the day they got out. Later on, Wade hired Emmet in the kitchen, and it seems like Wade's grooming Emmet to take over the diner. Jesse and Anthony's story didn't turn out as well. They got popped again for armed robbery about six months ago and are now over in Walpole. This time for a couple years.

The guys made a big deal of me stepping in that day, but I'm no Mahatma Gandhi, I'm no MLK. I just didn't want Wade or Wade's Diner to get all shot up, with windows shattered and hot bacon grease spilled and bloody bodies lying everywhere. Where would I go for breakfast?

Sandisfield: A Protest March and a Dinner

They were a funny little band. Maybe twenty of them, though the numbers went up and down as the march progressed. They had no support van, no infrastructure, they were just a group of people who depended on Providence to take them where they wanted to go, which was Sandisfield, Massachusetts, where they fully expected to be arrested. And Providence did indeed succor them. Everywhere they stopped, food miraculously appeared. Beds were offered, or at least space for them to stretch out their sleeping bags and their thin, tough Ensolite® pads, and facilities for them to shower and make ready for the next day's hike. Some of them were Quakers. Some were Unitarian Univeralist (UU) types.

Some of them, you couldn't have said what they were. Seekers, mostly. Seekers who had attached themselves to this cause, of stopping a needless and expensive pipeline from cutting through some of the most beautiful New England old growth forest left in the world. They stopped at churches, Quaker Friends meetinghouses, and sometimes private homes, ranging from millionaires' mansions to aging hippies' ramshackle houses. Sometimes they fed on adzuki beans and rice, sometimes on lavish chicken dinners with wine, French bread, and dessert trays. They didn't care. They were on a mission, joyfully and for the most part uncomplaining. Some of them had been on multiple marches. Some were first-timers. It didn't matter. The walking tired them out so much there was very little bickering, and the Friends among them quelled the rest.

They came to our home around four in the afternoon, twenty-six miles into a long day's walk from Huntington, down Routes 20 and 23, across the top of the Otis Reservoir, along Route 8 through the Tolland state forest, and finally into Sandisfield on Route 57. Tomorrow was the big day, arriving at the action site just a couple miles down the road. We were the last stop on the tour, and everybody was ready to celebrate. My wife made a big pasta–with-veggies dinner for 35, the marchers plus some of our activist neighbors like old Tom Lewis who owned a fruit orchard on the pipeline route. Ben's wife Becky (yep, Tom and Becky) brought dessert. A few other folks brought salads and chips and salsa and some cases of beer. We cleared everything out of the living room and used every chair in the house plus some folding chairs brought in, and blank doorframes on sawhorses at each end of our dining room table, to make a makeshift table like you might find in an old castle, long and low, with seats on both sides. Yes, sit-down dinner for 35. We were mighty proud of ourselves, but our contribution paled next to the commitment of those foot-weary people who lined the table that evening.

The group had no official leader but the unofficial head of the march was an activist from Maine named Jason O'Connor. He had stood in front of a bulldozer like an American Tiananmen Square-man at a potential refining facility in Rockport until the authorities caved and rescinded their building permit. He was a real hero— quiet, unassuming, a true Friend who let others speak before he did. He was thin, with a shaggy beard and soft yet piercing eyes, a rounded nose and lanky limbs. He wore the mantle of leader lightly, but I could see that the others loved him and looked up to him. Once they got settled in our great room, with pads laid down and sleeping bags rolled out, they had a long meeting of just themselves, presumably to go over strategy for tomorrow's protest. They had all undergone non-violent resistance training. Everything about them was peaceful—their road weariness, their Friends-style meeting methodology. They reminded me of a clowder of cats, cozying up to each other contentedly. In the fall weather they were dressed in a funky assortment of sweaters, hoodies, and jeans, with the occasional tie-dye T-Shirt or ones with anti-nuke and anti-pipeline slogans. In an odd dichotomy, as a group they felt both irreverent and beautifully reverent. They related to their elders not as mentors but as peers, with gentleness and a certain humorous detachment. They'd all heard stories about the Sixties, the antiwar protests, the sense of excitement and change in the air. They respected the past, but they were focused on the present. They were happy if you joined them, but it didn't matter. They were a committed force deep in the here and now but also facing forward into the future.

Our house was technically in the Berkshires but we were pretty far south of Greylock or any of the other Berkshire peaks. We grew sunflowers and had an apiary. I'd retired from my tech business and was a gentleman farmer. My wife ran a B&B out of two rooms in the house, but that was seasonal, and now it was November and nobody was coming to Sandisfield unless they were going to get arrested. The pipeline protest had been good for some businesses. The local coffee shop/bakery reported a pretty good season, with protesters, press, law enforcement, and tourists all frequenting the place, sometimes at the same time, for the home-made granola and local maple syrup, and the sugar donuts. But this dinner was just us locals and the protesters. It wasn't a town hall meeting. It was a meal in support of this motley crew of young people, along with a few arthritic oldsters who provided wisdom and comic relief in equal measure.

At dinner the talk was of nonviolence as a prelude to getting arrested. The young people were idealistic in the way we had been in the Sixties. More than one of us thought back to the days when we would have proudly marched with them, now in protest of a needless expansion of the antiquated and doomed fossil fuel industry. Our neighbor Ebenezer (everyone called him "Z") Buckhart came. A widower, he ran a small farm on his own without his helpmate of forty-five years, Martha, who'd passed away two years ago. Tall, slightly skeletal in appearance, with a hawk face and a white shock of hair on one side like Robert Frost, Z was one of those guys you think could walk out of the twenty-first century and back into the early 19th- or even 18th-century with no problem. I never saw him out of his farmer overalls and plaid work shirt. He didn't think much of the protesters, but he didn't think much of the government, either. He came to meet the young people personally. He wanted to make his own judgment about them. After a couple hours of listening to them, he stood up and declared his support:

"I came here looking to find some reason to oppose you, but I have to say, you've turned me. Tomorrow I'll fetch me a sign and stand next to you, if that's okay with you?" A chorus of assent met his utterance. Jason O'Connor put his arm around the ruddy-face elderly man, who stiffened but didn't shy away. They clinked bottles, "Z" drinking a "hahd cidah" from West County up in Colrain, and Jason working on a local IPA.

The next morning, we supplied jugs of coffee and my wife served up home-made muffins. Our neighbors brought in eggs and bacon and made piles of pancakes. The marchers assembled slowly for the final miles into Sandisfield. Nobody expected violence or even verbal conflict. They would sit down in front of the gate to the pipeline site. The police would tell them to move. They'd refuse. The police would arrest them gently and politely, on grounds of blocking traffic which made it an illegal protest. Their ACLU lawyer would bail them all out a few hours later and that would be that. That was the way it was supposed to go. We walked the first mile with them, and then most of us locals turned back to get our cars. A couple hours later we drove to the protest site. It had all the trappings of a construction site-- hillside behind the work zone stripped bare. Pipes came out of the ground, with caps and large wheels for turning valves. Men in hard hats and neon-colored vests stood around by their pickup trucks. Heavy equipment, bulldozers, backhoes, and a bucket shovel sat idle. A couple of burly security guys, obviously not from around here, stood guard at the gate. They were unarmed. These protests had been going on for years now, as the oil company's pipeline application wound its weary way through the federal bureaucracy. We parked a couple hundred yards from the gate where the protest was happening, and walked up the road to it. At that instant everything went crazy.

My wife and I tried to piece it together from our collective memories, but it still came through as a series of waves, with troughs, crests, and disorganized but fluid repetitiveness:

Wave 1—a man burst out of the woods in full combat gear and camouflage. He was shouting something about America, but honestly, I can't recall if he was yelling that he loved America or hated it. He was raising one of several semi-automatic files he had slung around his neck. It could easily have been another mass-shooting massacre except just as the shooter got ready to mow down the protesters (or was it the cops), bystander Ralph

Sokolski, sixty-eight-year-old Vietnam Vet, had a momentary flashback.

Wave 2—Ralph hurled himself at the guy and knocked him down. The cops swarmed on him. Not a shot was fired, thank God! The protesters, some visibly shaken, a few using bandannas to wipe tears away, formed themselves into a tight ring to talk and support one another.

Wave 3—The protesters broke the ring and Jason O'Connor announced the protest was over and everybody started to pack up and leave. The cops, busy with the lunatic would-be shooter, were grateful, and I even heard one of them say "See ya down at the dinah" as a red-eyed protester walked past.

The shooter turned out to be a psychopathic loner from out of state. The protests continue to this day, even as the pipeline construction goes on.

Brimfield: Conned by an Antique

Three times a year Gordy Lawson drove up from his modest apartment off East Fordham Road near the Bronx Zoo to attend the Brimfield Antique Show. It was more of a gigantic flea market than a true antique show. It allowed him to cut out the expensive stuff and focus on the pieces he could pick up for a song, and sell to the wealthy. He never sold anything at the show. Too many experts, who could tell his reclaimed wood pieces from the real thing, his poorly made copies from originals. He was a private seller, not a buyer or a trader. The truth was, Gordy didn't know that much about antiques. He'd grown up in the Bronx in the era of Chinet plates and bowls, beanbag chairs, and avocado and orange color schemes. He was half Puerto Rican and half black, but could pass for white and did so almost whenever he left the hood, or whenever it was convenient or he thought it would lead to a sale. But he wasn't above playing the race card and coming across as a naïve black man in over his head with a load of possibly stolen goods that he wanted some eager and morally bankrupt rich person to take off his hands. Gordy was a light-skinned black man with green eyes, a look that many women found entrancing, and that came in handy in his business also.

Gordy was a first-class con man. He'd tried his hand at various schemes over the years: phony real estate transactions, credit card skimming, the whole Nigerian prince thing on the internet, but he'd found his sweet spot in antiques. Part of the reason for this choice of cons was that people he sold to wanted to be conned. They wanted to believe that the stuff he peddled was real, and not fake. They coveted antique tables and dressers. Gordy learned how to drill wormholes and carve distress marks onto, and replace the pasteboard backings of the dressers with real wood. Sure, there were experts who could tell his stuff was counterfeit at a glance, but they weren't his market. He could smell them out and avoid them easily. No, his market was rich people who wanted to pretend they lived in a real old New England farm-house and furnish it with antiques, even if that farmhouse had radiant heating in the floor, electronically opened garage doors, and a hot tub on the porch. They wanted the look. Some of them didn't even care if the stuff was a sham as long as it *looked* authentic. The other part of why Gordy favored faux antiques over any other form of scam is that it brought him in contact with these rich bastards, gave him entree into their world, the expensive restaurants where he met them, the homes they occupied, the cars they drove.

This trip was different. Six inches of February snow made the driving tricky. There were no shows on, no tents or booths set up in the empty, snow-covered fields. He was making the trip to meet one customer at the Inn down the road from the town of Brimfield. It was one of those places you can find all over New England, a historic building with small rooms furnished with antiques, and a restaurant that makes old-fashioned New England dinners: bread on a bread board, butter in little ceramic tubs, iceberg lettuce salads, prime rib or beef stew entrees. Not at all like the trendy, expensive restaurants Gordy frequented in the City. But the roaring fire in an anteroom where you could have a drink before dinner and admire the historical paintings and sit on real antique chairs was a good setting for a sale.

Genevieve Lansing was waiting for him by the fire in the lobby. He was immediately taken by her looks—blonde hair swept back, patrician nose, small ears, lively eyes, impeccable taste in clothes. She was wearing a light blue chiffon dress that was cut modestly just below the knee and covered with a wool throw over the shoulders, and killer shoes with high but not ridiculously high heels. The perfect trophy wife look. Refined, a little daring, but not scandalous. Genevieve had contacted Gordy after seeing a cherry wood desk on his website. The original owner was reputed to be Elbridge Gerry, fifth vice president of the United States under James

Madison, and a signer of the Constitution. She'd requested a personal meeting to see the desk and probably purchase it. Though the ask was a bit unusual, Gordy decided to honor it.

Genevieve was the trophy wife of silver-haired hedge fund manager Mark Lansing. She was thirty years his junior. No longer a young woman, she was at an age where her beauty was elegant, refined, mature. Gordy had booked a table for dinner. He would show her the piece later. He was tempted to take her arm immediately but resisted, attempting to maintain the cool reserve of a successful businessman. Dinner was slightly awkward because they had no common acquaintances and traveled in different worlds though they both lived in New York. But both were eager to make the connection work, for different reasons.

At a dessert of Indian pudding the talk turned to the purpose of their meeting, the antique desk. Gordy had brought pictures. The piece itself was in the trunk of his car but he didn't tell her that yet. He wanted to gauge her true interest before he showed it to her. It was a little scratched and beat-up looking. In truth the desk was a throw-in with another purchase he'd made at the fall show, and he hadn't had time to fully vet it yet. He hadn't even posted a price for it on his website, but he knew that money was no object for Genevieve Lansing. And he didn't want to disappoint her. Genevieve took the pictures from him and look at them with intense interest.

"It's lovely. Does it have a secret drawer?"

"Several."

"Delightful. And can you verify its provenance?"

"I have papers documenting that it was in the posses-
sion of Gerry family descendants until about thirty years
ago. Since then it's changed hands a couple times." This
was a lie, of course. The papers were forgeries.

"When can I see it?"

"After dinner. I brought it with me."

"Wonderful."

When the bill came, Genevieve looked about her and
said: "Oh dear. I left my purse in the car. I'll just go out
and get it."

"I'll get this," Gordy answered. He always let the buyer
pay. It was one of the perks he enjoyed, but he was taken
by the charm of the woman and put down his titanium
card without hesitation. Once the bill was paid, Gordy
suggested that he could bring the desk up to his room
and she could look at it there, but Genevieve demurred.

"Where is the piece now?"

"In my car."

"Why don't you bring it into the anteroom? I'm sure
the Inn management won't mind."

Gordy thought this was slightly odd, but he understood why she wouldn't want to come to his room. He
didn't bother to put on a coat, but just went out and
opened the back of his SUV and lugged the small desk in.
It was a narrow escritoire, quite small and light, with
spindly legs, not a full desk. Gordy was pleased because
the fire in the oversized hearth in the anteroom made the
cherry wood of the desk glow with a deep, honeyed
gleam. Genevieve walked around the piece with a
practiced eye. After examining the piece for a couple
minutes, she turned to him and said:

"I'll take it."

"Excellent." He had never told her the price, which he hadn't set yet. Gordy calculated quickly and named a sum that would show him a reasonable profit. She didn't haggle.

"I had my purse with me after all. Would you like a check or do you have a way to process a credit card?"

"I do." Gordy had purchased one of those little square devices that allowed him to take credit cards through his iPhone. It was so much faster and avoided any issues over disgruntled customers who put stops on checks. He swiped her card and even printed her a receipt with a little handheld printer.

"Thank you," she said. "Now if you'll just help me move the desk into my car?"

Gordy was caught off guard. "You aren't staying here?"

"Oh no. Too louche. I'm staying—" she named a very fancy, very expensive hotel a few miles down the road.

"Of course." Gordy was disappointed. He had thought for a moment that there might have been—that was why he hadn't asked for more for the piece—but no, it was impossible, she was out of his league. He started to lift the desk to bring it outside, but she stopped him with a regal wave of a hand.

"Wait. First, I'd like to show you something, Gordy Lawson."

"Oh?" He didn't like the way she'd addressed him by his full first and last name.

"Yes. And tell you something. My husband Mark Lansing is a descendant of Elbridge Gerry."

"Oh?" An uncomfortable feeling was starting to take hold of Gordy Lawson.

"Yes. He'll remember this desk well. It sat in the library in his parents' home for many years. When he was a child he delighted in playing with the secret drawers."

"Oh?" Gordy's mind raced. Where was this going? Was she going to bust him for selling a fake?

"Yes. And, bad little boy, he carved his initials into the bottom of one of the drawers."

"Oh?" Gordy wondered if she'd called the police already.

"Yes. It was this one, I believe." She reached in beneath where the desk had an overhanging shelf with slots for letters and papers, and pulled a hidden handle that released a narrow spring-loaded drawer tucked into the false back of the desk. The drawer popped out smoothly. Pulling the drawer all the way out of its space, she turned it over, and there were the initials ML, scratched in a childish hand.

"I see," said Gordy.

"Do you?" Genevieve asked. "This is the original."

"I see." Gordy's mind was racing. Why hadn't he checked out the piece properly before he'd sold it? He'd bought it so cheaply last fall that he'd just assumed it was an imitation. A bad error, one that might even cost him his freedom if she had contacted the police.

"It's worth much more than what you charged me."

Now it was Gordy's turn to be irate. "What difference does that make to you? You have all the money you'll ever need."

"It was a matter of principle. I shouldn't have to overpay for something that never should have left the family in the first place. It'll make a nice present for my husband's birthday."

"*Bitch!*" Gordy thought, but he merely nodded that he understood. The con man had gotten conned. Outwardly obsequious now, he carried the desk to her car, a top of the line Mercedes SUV. She clicked open the rear hatch with an electronic button on her key. He lifted the desk into place and shut the door. As she opened the driver's side door to get in, he started to protest that he hadn't done anything wrong, but she waved him to silence again:

"Don't worry, little man, you haven't broken any laws. You thought you were selling me a worthless copy. How could you have known?"

He wanted to say "*Go to hell!*" or something worse, but he was afraid that she would expose him to the world and ruin him. Desperate to regain a little of his dignity, he reached into his suit jacket inside pocket while saying:

"May I give you my card? Perhaps—" but she ignored him, shut the door, and started the engine. He stepped away as she backed out of the parking space and drove off. He shivered from the cold, went back inside and ordered brandy, and sat by the fire for a long time before he went up to his room.

West Brookfield: Four Women

Paul Finster was a historian writing a book about central Massachusetts. He'd settled on the Brookfields as his territory for historical exploration. His mother, a feminist activist, had inspired him to narrow his subject matter to the lives of two women: Bathsheba Spooner and Lucy Stone. Bathsheba Spooner was a criminal who was hanged on July 2nd, 1778, during the American revolution, before a crowd of 5,000 people in Worcester's Washington Square, out front of the current Union Station train depot, for murdering her drunken and abusive husband. Lucy Stone became the first woman from Massachusetts to earn a college degree, a feminist before that term was invented, a suffragist and an abolitionist. It had struck Paul as remarkable that these two such opposite women should be the most prominent females to have come from this little town in the center of the state, and as a historian he was drawn to their stories. Four towns: Brookfield, East Brookfield, West Brookfield, North Brookfield. (There is no South Brookfield.) Two women. He'd taken a room in the old inn in the center of Brookfield, and spent his days poring over books, maps, documents, photos, drawings and physical artifacts housed in wooden cases with glass covers in the Quaboag Historical Society located in the old West Brookfield Boston & Albany train station.

Historians were the nerds before the high-tech kids took over. Paul Finster wore glasses, wore a bland, slightly bewildered look most of the time. His wavy brown hair and even, symmetrical features would have made him handsome if he'd let any of his inner complexity show through. Instead he blundered softly through life, sad and alone. He'd resigned himself to being a lifelong bachelor. What little pleasure he enjoyed came from his work, and from food. He'd taught himself to be a pretty decent cook, and treated himself to expensive restaurants once in a while to see what new things were coming onto menus in modern cuisine. He'd even experimented with foams and smoke and gels. Out here in the Brookfields, culinary delights were rare. Pizza, bad Chinese, and old-fashioned "American tavern" cooking dominated. He'd taken to driving into Worcester on occasion, where there were a few decent places. In the mornings he'd found a coffee shop that had okay coffee and homemade scones.

Karen Strozek, the librarian/curator of the Quaboag Historical Society Museum, had graciously agreed to let Paul into the museum every day for two weeks. It was usually open only on the first Saturday of every month. She puttered around for the first day, making sure he wasn't going to walk off with anything valuable. Once she realized he was a serious historian, she just unlocked the front door in the morning and left him to mull over old newspapers, journals, and diaries. She only came back in the evening to lock up.

On Friday at the end of the first week, Karen hung around while he was gathering up his papers, and surprised him by inviting him out for dinner the next night, Saturday. He was taken aback and only said yes because he didn't know how else to answer. Paul found her a bit forward. She had picked the place already, the Salem Cross Inn in West Brookfield, just a couple miles up the road from the museum. He checked out the menu online and found that it offered "traditional American fare" and "colonial cuisine." He couldn't help but be a little bit excited by the idea of going out to dinner with a woman. The last time he'd dated anyone was in college, before grad school years ago.

The Salem Cross Inn was a charming old New England building with a tavern, lots of dark wood everywhere, butter served in crocks, bread on a breadboard, a full-on anachronism except now the owners promised "locally sourced" vegetables and meat. Paul had chosen to wear his tweed jacket with the elbow patches—he fit right in. The only thing he lacked was a pipe. Karen showed up in a racy little number not at all the quaint librarian Paul expected. She dyed her hair blonde and wore this tight-fitting dress that accentuated her slim but curvy body. She didn't wear glasses. Her eyes were sharp, deep blue, and inquiring. They sat on authentic New England hard benches at a corner table and ordered drinks, a merlot for Paul and a dirty martini for Karen.

"So, what have you been doing in my shelves this past week?"

"I'm researching the lives of two women from Brookfield."

"Oh? Who?"

"I doubt you will have heard of them. One is Bathsheba Spooner."

"Bathsheba? Oh, sure, I know her. I'm a feminist, like her. I believe in free love, like her."

Paul did a quick double-take. He'd never heard anyone call Bathsheba Spooner a feminist. Lucy Stone, sure, but the convicted adulteress and murderer Bathsheba?

"You're married?" He assumed so. He'd noticed a ring.

"Yeah."

"Uh, what does your husband think of that?"

"He tolerates it. He thinks I wouldn't actually do anything. He's wrong, though." Karen's blue eyes settled on Paul, challenging him.

Paul's face flushed. He didn't know where to look. This was the history he was studying come alive in the most improbable and personal way. He tried to make a joke. "So, you consider yourself like Bathsheba? Are you going to murder your husband?"

Karen laughed a little too loudly. "Maybe. I have no plans to get hung in Worcester, though. Yes, I consider Bathsheba Spooner a feminist. Bathsheba was an independent spirit. She refused to service her weak, alcoholic husband, who took to seducing the servant women, and she herself took a teenage lover who participated in the murder. Today a good lawyer might get her off on grounds of abuse and threats on her life by her husband, but back then she was the daughter of a confirmed Tory who was run out of town by his neighbors during the War of Independence. She was sentenced to death by a jury of twelve men who refused to believe the obvious fact that she was pregnant and deserved a stay of execution."

Paul was stunned. This woman knew as much about Bathsheba Spooner as he did. Maybe more.

"Who's the other one?"

"What?"

"You said there were two."

"Oh, Lucy Stone."

"Lucy Stone. And you thought I wouldn't have heard of these two women? That's very insulting, you know."

"I'm sorry."

"If you'd looked at our website, which I helped create, you'd know we give out a Lucy Stone award every year."

"I'm sorry," Paul said again. He felt like crawling under the table.

"You must think we're real po-dunkers out here in the Brookfields, huh? Where do you live? Brooklyn?"

"Cambridge."

"Figures."

The drinks came. Despite the tension in the air, they clinked glasses automatically and drank. Paul tried to make amends.

"I'm very impressed with the museum, and with your knowledge of what's in it."

"Thank you." A short interval of quiet passed. Paul assumed Karen was thinking about walking out on the dinner date. Karen broke the awkward silence: "Lucy could walk into a women's rights meeting today and lead it. She was like a hundred and seventy-five years ahead of her time."

"I agree," Paul said hurriedly.

"The only difference between Lucy and me is that I believe in free love like Bathsheba, and Lucy Stone didn't."

"I see." Paul couldn't think of anything remotely appropriate to say.

"What about you?"

"What about me?"

"What do you believe in?"

"Uh, I believe in romantic love, I guess. A man and a woman."

"Oh god, don't tell me you're against gay marriage?"

"No no, it's fine, I mean, it's just not romantic the way I think of it."

"You probably think online dating apps are no good either."

"You're right, I do."

"That's very romantic. Naïve and old-fashioned, but romantic. Listen, after dinner why don't we go to your room in the Brookfield Inn and screw our brains out?"

All the color drained from Paul's face and then rushed back in blotches of red. "Okay, yes." He paused for a minute. "Do we have to have dinner?"

Karen laughed again, softer now, lascivious. "That's the romantic part, silly." She took his hand and sucked his little finger. "I'm having the prime rib. Grrr!"

During the meal Paul recovered sufficiently to talk about his love of cooking, and to ask Karen more questions about Bathsheba Spooner and Lucy Stone and other colorful women from Brookfield. All the while, though he was wondering if it was safe to do what he was about to do, have an affair with a married woman. Somewhere between the main course and dessert he managed to ask:

"So, is your husband out of town?"

"No, he's home."

"Won't he wonder?"

Karen batted her eyelashes at Paul, renewing her provocation. "I told you, he doesn't believe I would do anything. Look, let's get this all out of the way. I'm not leaving him for you. I just want to have a little fun and give you some too, because it looks like you need it."

"Great."

That night, and three times over the next week while Paul stayed in the Brookfield Inn, Karen came to his room and gave him and herself "a little fun." She told him that he was a good lover and that he just needed to slow down and take his time. He followed her instructions. During the day she ignored him; she arrived to open the museum and then disappeared until it was time to close up. They had one more dinner at the Inn. Karen was careful to tell anyone who asked (it was a small town, after all, and she couldn't help but run into people she knew at dinner) that she was just being a gracious host to the "goofy history nut" who was spending his days inside the old train station. At the end of the second week Paul had used up all the funds from the small American Antiquarian Society grant he'd been awarded for the research. He made preparations to leave. Karen came by on the Saturday of his departure, but they didn't go to bed. Instead they had bad coffee in his room and sat awkwardly facing each other at an angle on the old four-poster bed.

"I've never met anyone like you," Paul said.

"And you won't, ever again." Paul didn't know if she meant that he'd never see her again, or never meet another character like her. Both interpretations turned out to be true.

"You helped me, a lot," he said.

"You helped me, too. That was my first time."

"Uh?"

"First time trying out free love. It won't be the last time. Bathsheba would be proud of me. And Lucy too, in her own way. I'm marching in the women's march next week in Boston."

Paul's head swirled upwards like a kite suddenly let go. No one had ever talked to him like this, about subjects like this. How was he going to go back to his pathetic bachelor life in Cambridge after this affair? He had a feeling everything about his life was about to change. He wasn't even sure he wanted to be a historian any more. They parted at the door to his room.

"Send me a copy of your article, or book, or whatever it is, will you?"

"I'll send it to the museum."

"Good idea. We'll include it in our local history section."

"It's all local history, isn't it?"

"Ya got me there, bud." Karen was pleased. She'd woken up this guy. Paul beamed too.

"Bye."

"Bye."

Paul drove away in his compact rental car that morning.

Two years later Paul was sitting in his kitchen relaxing over one of his gourmet breakfasts. Eggs benedict with salmon and his own Hollandaise sauce. He was listening to the morning news. A woman in Brookfield had been shot by her husband in a murder-suicide. It was Karen Strozek. Paul dropped his fork with a clatter and groaned. His wife Lalit looked up, her dark eyes questioning. Paul was pale. He told her the person on the news was the librarian who had helped him when he was doing research for the book that had made his name as a historian, the book that had helped bring him and Lalit together. After those idyllic weeks in the Brookfields, Paul had forced himself to try a few dating techniques. He didn't do so well with the online dating sites, but had success with the slightly snobby personals in the back pages of the *New York Review of Books*— *"Handsome academic with culinary skills seeking a woman with an educated palate, etc."* He'd found a partner in Lalit, an East Indian female mathematician in her final year of grad school at MIT. She read his book in draft form and helped him edit it. They were very happy together. She knew nothing of Karen Strozek except what Paul had just told her, that Karen had helped him with his research.

Apparently Karen had grown less discreet. After her first affair with Paul she had had "a little fun" with increasing frequency. The numerous affairs had become common town gossip, and when her husband finally heard, he went mad with jealousy and anger, killed her and then shot himself in the head. Paul had never told anyone about what had happened during his weeks in West Brookfield, and he and Karen had never communicated again. It was like a dream. Paul decided to attend Karen's funeral. He wore a dark suit and stayed at the back during the service in the local church, and talked to no one. Then he followed the cortege out to the local cemetery. Despite the horrific and tragic end to their lives, Karen and her husband were going to be buried side by side in the plots they'd selected and paid for in advance. His funeral had been delayed by legal proceedings. Karen was laid into the ground first, on a hot, muggy, dreary rainy day in August. The Brookfield Cemetery held graves from all the way back to the early 1700s, including that of Joshua Spooner, husband of Bathsheba, who is buried in an unmarked grave somewhere in Worcester. As a scholar, Paul knew that he wouldn't find Lucy Stone's grave here. In addition to being the first woman from Massachusetts to receive a college degree, Lucy Stone was the first person in Massachusetts to be cremated. Always in the vanguard, she insisted on six men and six as pallbearers when her cremated remains were interred in Forest Hills Cemetery. But her last wish, to be remembered as Lucy "Stone," was not honored, and her gravestone bears her husband's name: "Blackwell."

The service was quick and there were few mourners. No one remembered Paul from those two weeks two years ago. Why should they? He'd spent almost all his time in the museum or in his room at the Brookfield Inn. Paul hung around until everyone had left, even leaving himself and then returning a half-hour later so as not to be noticed when he visited the new grave.

He stood in the still air of the cemetery, weeping silently. He owed this woman so much he could hardly express it. Paul's slim history text with the dull title: *Bathsheba Spooner and Lucy Stone: Two Women of Brookfield* had been published by a university press a few months before and had sold surprisingly well for an academic book, perhaps because of its feminist bent and its celebration of two women ahead of their times. It was very popular in the Brookfields. Paul had turned down an opportunity to come out and do a book-signing. Karen had left the museum by the time the book was published and had started a new career as a real estate agent. The replacement who invited him was an elderly woman, a sour old thing who just wanted to make money for the museum. She was as unlike Karen as any woman could be.

Paul could never forget how this now murdered woman had transformed his life. What if he had insisted on her leaving her husband? Would she have been spared? Or would he have become the victim? Or the cuckold? It was never meant to be. She had showed him the way to open up. Now she was gone.

He took a single rose out of its thin paper and plastic wrapping and laid it on the fresh earth, glanced at the as yet undug plot where her husband would soon lie, and removed from his coat pocket a copy of *Bathsheba Spooner and Lucy Stone: Two Women of Brookfield*, with its mysterious dedication:

"For K— a woman like the two in this book."

He placed the thin volume on the fresh turned earth next to the flower and left, not looking back and never visiting again. His wife Lalit was no fool. When the book came out, she had not asked about the inscription, and Paul had never volunteered its meaning. Now she connected the words with the recent events in West Brookfield, but she never said a word about it to Paul.

Hatfield: The Jamaicans and a Missing Daughter

They come in April when the weather is still decidedly un-Jamaica like. They stay until December. In between, they work twelve-hour days, six days a week. They live together in a little shack off River Road in Hatfield, up to a dozen of them, in circumstances that are worse than their living conditions at home. They all have old English names like Browning, Winchester, and Taylor. They work the fields of Hatfield in their methodical, unhurried, but effective way. And they change us, by being here. I was working as a foreman on the Clear River Farm in Hatfield when I first met them. I was jobbing in for Eddie Matulewicz's son Damon. I'd had a few jobs like that before, overseeing Mexicans or Guatemalans during the growing season. It was a pretty common thing up here in the Valley—there just wasn't enough seasonal help without the migrant workers. But the Jamaicans were— different. First off, they accepted me immediately like I was just one of them, out there working in the fields. Which I was. The Mexicans, though friendly, didn't receive as openly, nor the Guatemalans. Maybe it was the language barrier. Though the first few days I had trouble understanding the lilting patois of Jamaican speech, after a while I thought I was getting the accent too. I played bones (dominoes) with them, drank their Red Stripe beer, ate their jerked chicken. At night I could go home to my air-conditioned house while they slept with the windows open to the stifling humidity. But we got along great, and I was as happy with that crew as I've ever been with any group of men who worked the fields with me. This Connecticut River valley bottom land is some of the finest in the world. We call the dirt "Hadley loam," and we call the asparagus, which used to grow wild all over the valley and now is a major crop, "Hadley grass."

I've been an idiot a few times in my life, and this was one of them. I mean, it was all happening under my nose. And I knew none of the Jamaicans would ever—ah, but I was an idiot.

One night toward the end of the growing season we decided to have a barbeque and dance to celebrate the harvest. We cleared out a space in the barn where we trimmed and boxed the vegetables, and set up a sound system. We couldn't afford a band, but we had lots of reggae CDs. My wife Alice cooked up a bunch of chicken and some of the guys made rice and beans and cabbage. There was lots of Red Stripe, and some Dragon Stout and some Yardy Shandy. Neighbors came, and after a while we had fifty or sixty people in the barn, dancing and eating and enjoying themselves by the light of candles in paper bags. My family came, my wife Alice and my daughter Lily. Lily's a pretty girl with blonde hair, and a slight limp from being born with one leg shorter than the other. She brought her boyfriend Frank, a local kid whose dad ran one of the few dairy farms left in Massachusetts. Frank's last name was Mulligan. A few of the Jamaicans fancied themselves as golfers and Frank's name caused them no end of glee.

"Hey, Mulligan! Do ova, mon. Do ova!" they would shout at him when they saw him walking with Lily along the edge of the fields where they weeded and hoe' d and watered. They made fun of my name too—Harvey Freeman. They called me 'Hardly FreeMon' because they saw how hard I worked, which they found unusual for a white man. They were used to overseers who stayed in the shade and let them do all the tough stuff, the back-breaking hand-weeding. We were an organic farm, no pesticides. There were plenty of weeds. All of it required lots of bending over, crouching, tugging, and repetitive stress motions.

A couple times during the night I saw Lily dancing with the Jamaican kid Westley. He was the youngest of the crew, probably not much older than my daughter. I didn't think anything of it at the time. Lily's always gotten along with the Jamaican crew. They treated her with respect as the daughter of the boss. A couple hours into the dance I was called away to look at a broken irrigation pipe and when I came back the thing was winding down and people were putting the barn back in order for the next day's work. My wife and Lily were gone, I assumed they'd gone home. But when I got back to the house my wife was up and on the phone. Lily was missing. She'd asked to stay when her mother left, and hadn't returned home. Alice was on the line with the Hatfield police, who were telling her they couldn't look for her until it was really a missing persons case, that she should wait until morning and then come in and file a report if Lily didn't show up. Obviously, they thought it was just a teenager pushing the boundaries; it wasn't even midnight.

The next morning Lily still hadn't come home. Neither Alice nor I had slept a minute. I'd driven up and down River Road for two hours looking for her. We went to the local police station. They were politely skeptical but took our information and issued a "Be on the Lookout" (BOLO) alert. There was nothing more I could do. I went to work. We were harvesting a field of cabbage, fierce work in the August sun. Right away I saw the crew was down a couple people, including the kid Westley. I called Taylor over.

"You're short a couple men," I said.

"Yas, boss. Too much shandy for sure."

"Where's young Westley?"

Something in my tone must have tipped off Taylor about my suspicions. His usually open and friendly face assumed a mask of indifference.

"Him? Can't hold his liquor, mon. He's sleeping it off. He'll be round by noon."

"Have him come see me."

"Yas, boss."

My wife called me while I was in the fields. No news. She was in a panic, but what could I do? Harvest cabbages, was about all. The day dragged on. Westley never showed up. I sought out Taylor again. He was the informal foreman. Officially Foreman was my job, but the Jamaicans took their orders from Taylor.

"What's going on, Taylor?"

"What you mean, boss?"

"Cut the crap, man. Did he run off with my daughter?"

"You mean the lame girl?" He knew perfectly well who I meant.

"Hey, that's my daughter you're talking about."

"She lame, ain't she?"

I had to admit she was. "Well, did he?"

"Who?"

"Westley."

"No, mon, no. Ya got it all wrong, mon." But he wouldn't say anything more. I couldn't tell if he was protecting Westley, or what the hell was going on. It was useless to question him further myself. I called the police, and told them to come. I said I thought my workers knew something about my daughter's disappearance. I thought they might have sent the town's lone detective, but instead they sent a squad car with a uniformed officer. This was soon after the president had ordered a crackdown on immigration, and I knew some of my guys were in the country illegally, but they didn't run, they just kept lopping the heads off the big purple cabbages, leaving the outer leaves, so that after the harvest the field looked like a windstorm had hit it. And it would stink pretty bad of rotting cabbage for a couple weeks. The cop was Joe Melnicky, somebody I'd grown up with and hung out with after high school. Built like the full-back/catcher/shot putter that he was, with an open face that didn't fit very well with his buzz cut and starched and buttoned up uniform. He shook his head and asked me to call the workers together, and he proceeded to interview them one by one while the others stood around. It was all *pro forma*, very brief, as if neither he nor the Jamaicans believed anything would come of it. Westley wasn't among them. When it was over, I walked Joe to his patrol car.

"They don't know anything, or if they do, they're not going to tell me."

"That's it, then? What about the kid who isn't here now, Westley?"

"What about him?"

"Like, maybe he ran off with my daughter?"

Joe gave me a funny look. "I don't think so, Harvey." But he didn't elaborate, and I didn't press him on it. "She'll turn up, Harvey. Just give it a little time. There hasn't been a serious crime in this town in years. I don't believe there's been one now, either."

It was like everybody knew something I didn't know. And they did.

Later the same day Immigration and Customs Enforcement (ICE) raided our farm wearing their blue jackets with bright yellow lettering. Just like when Patrolman Melnicky showed up, the Jamaicans didn't panic or flee. But this was much more serious for them than a local cop asking about a missing girl. They kept working until they were led away all of them, even the ones with legal visas or green cards. Westley wasn't among them. The ICE agents were reasonably polite, perhaps because the Jamaicans spoke English and didn't resist. No more cabbages were picked that day, or the next. I had to borrow some workers from a crew on another farm to get the crop in. They let Taylor stay because he had a valid work permit. He avoided me most of the morning, staying far out in a remote field where we had some tough to harvest berries growing along the edge in addition to squash and late season kale. When he came in for lunch I came up to him and asked him how the guys were doing.

"How you think, mon? They are sad, very sad. Some those men been comin' here for years. Now they can't any more. 'Twill be very tough on their families, that's for sure."

"I'm sorry this happened, Taylor."

"I'm sure you are, boss, I'm sure you are."

There was an awkward pause. Then Taylor looked me in the eyes and said: "She was just trying to get away."

"From who, Taylor?"

"From you, boss." Taylor had never spoken to me like that before. I knew he was angry about the ICE raid and his co-workers being sent back. And I was to blame, there could be no doubt, making a fuss over my daughter when she was just a young girl looking for freedom and a way out of the dreary rural life she imagined was her future. That afternoon we got a call from Lily. She was in a hotel in Boston. With Frank Mulligan. They were married. Like I said, I was an idiot. I told her to come home, that there wouldn't be any punishment, that we loved her. She said they would be back in the Pioneer

Valley in a couple weeks, they were going to take a road trip honeymoon to Florida and back, and then move into an apartment in North Hadley near the old dam. Okay, I could live with that. It was across the river, but not far away. Maybe they needed that big river as a natural separator. I didn't know. I didn't know anything. Westley showed up again a few days later. He'd been hiding out on Third Island down by the Sunderland Bridge, a regular Jamaican Huckleberry Finn. At the barn dance he'd just been being friendly, because he thought it was okay, he thought he was safe. Now he was afraid of getting shot by angry father (me), or worse, lynched for dancing with a lame white girl.

Six of the Jamaicans, the ones who didn't have any kind of visa at all, were sent back. We worked with a skeleton crew for the rest of the summer. It was hard on everyone. I was no longer welcome in the workers' house for bones and beer. I was the bad guy, the one who'd gotten their friends deported. I hadn't meant to be the villain in the piece, but that's the way it worked out. The next year none of the Jamaicans came, and I had to scramble to find enough people among the Mexicans and Guatemalans to bring in the crops. That winter I flew to Jamaica and begged them to come back, and told them I would make arrangements with the Jamaican government and the United States Government to assure they were protected from ICE. They appreciated the effort I'd made to come see them, but they didn't believe I could protect them. And they were probably right. They knew more about this, and farming, and life, than I would ever know.

I became a grandfather over that winter. Frank and Lily named their newborn boy Westley Mulligan.

A Book of Fields

Middlefield: A Visit to IT's Gravestone

The first part of Beka Smith's bike ride was a quarter mile of dangerous twists and turns down their gravel driveway, which meant an uphill as the last part of every ride. It made her wonder why she lived in the hilly country of Western Massachusetts, considering how much she like riding her bike. But her husband John liked the privacy of living in the woods, and she'd decided that as long as he was willing to look after the two kids a few times a week during the riding season, they'd stay where they were. When she got to the roadway she had several choices for easy, medium, and hard rides. Beka was a slim, fast rider. After tucking her short brown hair into her helmet, she could easily be mistaken for a man.

She loved the freedom the bicycle gave her. She crisscrossed the hills of Sheffield, New Marlborough, Chester, Sandisfield, and even down into northern Connecticut on weekend rides. One of Beka's favorites was to pedal out to the Mack Cemetery on Skyline Trail behind the town hall, which was an old elementary school converted to town offices. There was a bench where she could sit and enjoy that spectral silence that overtakes graveyards. The view was peaceful though not spectacular. There she would have a snack and drink some water. And there was one unique feature to the little village graveyard—set apart from the other graves at the edge of the north tree line behind the town building was a rough-hewn gravestone with only the letters "IT" carved into it. Even though Middlefield was a tiny little village, nobody in town knew or would admit to knowing who was buried there under the marker with just two letters on it. Many rumors had sprung up about the grave and the odd headstone—it was the resting place of a runaway slave, it was an adulteress whose name could not be put in writing, it was someone whose name could not be written because it would reveal a gruesome secret. Some believed the cemetery was haunted. "IT" had even made websites that tracked paranormal activity, and was considered one of those eccentric historic New England places to visit, though hardly anyone ever came there— Middlefield was too far from anything else to be a destination. Beka often had the place to herself. Even the town offices were closed most of the time.

One Sunday morning, however, as Beka was resting on the bench near the "IT" stone, a car pulled into the town hall parking lot. It wasn't an ordinary automobile--it looked like a Bentley or a Rolls Royce. Beka wasn't into cars and couldn't have said the difference. It was an older model, with rounded fenders sweeping curved lines from front to back, and protruding headlamps. The driver, in chauffeur's livery, hustled out of the driver's seat and opened the right-side back door of the car, and out stepped a woman in a black dress with a mantilla and old-fashioned mourning lace covering her face. Beka stood up immediately, though she wasn't sure why. It felt like she had fallen into a time warp or entered an alternate reality, but the woman and the chauffeur and the car were all very real. The woman in black walked with a black cane, haltingly, toward the "IT" grave. Beka was frozen in place, and could only nod when the woman passed without acknowledging her, the chauffeur in tow with a small basket (also black). The strange mourner reached the headstone and stopped. She crossed herself, and gestured imperiously to the chauffeur without turning her head to look at him. He withdrew a small spray of tiny blue flowers, something one could pick on a roadside, not get from a florist, and handed it to the woman, who stooped and placed it at the foot of the grave with delicate and painfully slow movements. Beka was paralyzed. She waited to see what would happen next. The woman stood for a long while head bowed, the chauffeur also immobile, the three of them including Beka forming a weird tableau. Finally, she turned to leave, the chauffeur striding ahead of her to open the door. As she passed by Beka this time, Beka spoke to her:

"Thank you," she said. She didn't know why, but it seemed the right thing to say. The woman came to a halt and faced her. The response came in a harsh whisper:

"For what, my dear?"

"I don't know. For keeping up this peaceful place, I guess."

"It's the least I could do."

Beka desperately wanted to ask who "IT" was, and what was the woman's connection to "IT," but she found herself unable to form the question. They stood awkwardly facing each other, Beka with a tight smile, the woman in black impenetrable beneath her lace veil.

"Enjoy the day," the woman said, and moved on, leaving Beka standing foolishly silent. As the antique luxury car pulled away she thought of writing down the license number, but it was too late, they were gone, and the silence of the graveyard reigned again. A few minutes passed. When Beka was sure they wouldn't return, she tiptoed over to the headstone and examined the flowers. There was no note, no card, nothing that would provide any more information about the identity of "IT" or of the mourner.

Afterward Beka always hoped she would see the mourning woman again, and even made a point of visiting the Mack Cemetery on her solitary rides both on the same day and time they'd met and on at different times and days. She never saw the ethereal woman in black again. Later in life Beka sometimes wondered if she'd dreamed the whole thing, but she had a tangible reminder that the meeting had really occurred: pressed beneath two plates of glass in her home was the posy of dried blue flowers she had taken from the grave after they'd wilted but before they had faded back into the earth.

Enfield: A Ghost in the Quabbin Reservoir

In the middle of the last century, the towns of Dana, Enfield, Prescott and Greenwich in Western Massachusetts were submerged by the construction of the Quabbin Reservoir. For seven years, the waters of the Quabbin rose behind dams and dikes. The reservoir was declared full of drinking water for Boston in June of 1946. Only one thing--they forgot about me.

I'd been living in an abandoned cellar hole in Enfield for a few years before the flooding. The townspeople were nice to me. They left cabbages and parsnips outside the hole every once in a while, and nobody minded when I chopped down a couple small oaks for firewood. I'd grown up in Enfield. Been a high school football star. Played in the school band. Dated a cheerleader. Busted a knee senior year so I never went to college on that scholarship B.C. offered me. I just hung around my dad's farm and drank too much. I couldn't serve in the army in the war and finally ended up a country bum, spending my nights down in that cellar hole with a bottle of cheap whiskey and roaming the bucolic countryside by day. I would sometimes help with the haying or the apple-picking in season. And that might have been the end of the story except when they cleared out everybody so that the water could come in, they forgot about me. Everybody left. I was the King of Enfield. I suppose I died, but it was hard to tell. My spirit mingled with the rising waters. I wandered through the sunken town, my old school, the church (missing only its steeple) where I was baptized, the deserted houses of my neighbors. I was free. Free to leave, but I never left. When the men from the state came sometimes to check on things, that's when I knew I was dead, because they couldn't see or hear me, but I could play little tricks on them, mess with their hair, fool with their surveying equipment, tangle their boat anchors.

Why had they done this? Why had they ruined our lovely valley, destroyed four towns, and moved everybody out? Just so the people of Boston could have drinking water—our drinking water, from our Swift River Valley? It didn't seem fair. The rest of the people in Prescott, Greenwich, Dana, and Enfield went on to new lives elsewhere. I stayed. I decided to make it my mission in death to haunt the administrators, surveyors, and water treatment workers. I wanted to force them to remember that once there had been a beautiful valley here, four thriving communities, a paradise that they had obliterated in water. Every year on June 22nd, the anniversary of the completion of the flooding in 1946, when the water crested over the spillway, and the reservoir was deemed finished, I try to do something a little special. This year on that date a guy came out to check the base of the Winsor Dam. Most of them just drive across the roadway on the top of the dam and look for leaks on the earthen embankment side, but this guy brought his scuba gear and dove down on the water side. Right into my demesne. As a spirit, I can do a little shape-shifting. I appeared to him first as a giant brookie. That got his attention. He couldn't believe it, and fumbled for the underwater camera he'd brought along to record any dam issue. Then I floated past him as myself, a bloated corpse. He tore at his breathing apparatus as if he thought he was suffering from hypoxia. It was hilarious, to me anyway. I'm an audience of one for myself. That should have been the end of it. But then he panicked, and grabbed at me, and I had to hold onto him. They dragged the reservoir for days but I kept his body under the water and away from the trolling nets and the divers they sent, and they never found him. He wasn't like me. His spirit didn't inhabit the place. The bass and pickerel and bullhead nibbled at his flesh until there was nothing but bones.

I'm still here.

A Book of Fields

North Brookfield: A Day at the Quaboag Quaffery

People came for the barbeque. They came for the little zoo out back with rabbits and goats the kids could pet. They came for the music, an everchanging cast of rockabilly, country jazz (if that's even a genre) and hardcore folky groups. But mostly they came for the beer, made with hops grown right on the farm. The Quabbin Quaffery was a success from the day it opened. They offered a variety of locally sourced beers but heavy on the New England IPAs. When they opened up a barbeque pit in the first summer, people flocked to the place. They set up a trebuchet in the fall and let people fling pumpkins at an old Ford truck they parked at the bottom of the swale behind the brewery.

On hot August weekend nights, the place is overrun with people drinking beer, eating barbeque, listening to music, and generally having a good time. It's a peaceful crowd despite the beer drinking. A few motorcycle groups come by, mostly oldsters, mostly couples, riding their shiny Harley hogs at a stately pace around New England. It's a mixed crowd. The servers are kids just out of college, and the brewers are young, nerdy, and totally into it. Some of the patrons are young enough to have young kids, hence the petting zoo, and some of the bands are under thirty. Millennials to Medicare recipients. And it's a warm, friendly, open, easy-going place. Most of the time.

The night The Blues Girls played was different. What is it about the blues? It brings out the nasty drunks, the bitter jilted boyfriends, the unlovable losers of the world. And when it's played by three witchy-looking post-punk rockers in black jeans and hoodies, well, things can get a little crazy. The Quaffery had expanded their summer space by putting up a big tent and placing picnic tables under it. The Blues Girls set up in a corner underneath the tent. They were the classic three-piece rock band-- guitar, bass, and drums. What they lacked in numbers they made up for in volume, using stacks of old Marshall amps bought at a second-hand music store. Their set was classic blues, from Robert Johnson down through Muddy Waters, Howling Wolf, and all their progeny in the rock world. Hard edged blues with extended guitar solos. Kathy Connors was the lead guitarist, a red-haired Irish banshee most people simply called Killer, from when she worked as a cook in a bar and didn't take any crap.

Waiters who lived in fear of her. She was stringy like
Gregg Allman, and often wore her hoodie with the sleeves
cut off to show her biceps. She did most of the singing
too, though they all sang three-part harmonies on some
of the choruses. The bass player was Nancy "Don't Call
Me Nan" Slawzarski, a short, attractive thickset blonde
with meaty hands and fingers covered in calluses from
plucking the strings of her electric bass. The drummer,
LaTonya Harris, was from Louisiana. She sported a big
Afro, and often wore a Zulu cotton-print dashiki shirt
over her black Levi's instead of a hoodie. With boundless
energy, she was crazy, like all drummers are. She never
stopped drumming. If you sat with her at a coffee shop
you got a continuous solo with straws as drumsticks and
feet constantly tapping. She anchored the group with a
deep, slow backbeat that had wisps of swamp smoke in
it. This band had magic to it, an indefinable quality that
made them exciting to listen to and watch, like a bomb
about to go off, unpredictable, veering and careening
from slow blues to end-of-*Freebird* wildness, sometimes
in the same song, like *Freebird*. They deserved to play in
bigger venues than the Quabbin Quaffery, but so far
success had eluded them.

It was late afternoon when The Blues Girls started to
play, kicking off the set with an old Elmore James slow
blues: *It Hurts Me Too*, only when LaTonya sang the
chorus in her Cajun twang it came out "*Hoits Me Too*."
People began to dance in front of the makeshift stage.
The sun slanted in, bathing everything in a thick late
summer afternoon light like Tupelo honey. The dancers
were sweating and trying not to spill their beers. The

band cranked it up for a second number, another slow blues, Guitar Slim's *The Things That I Used to Do*, but louder, with more guitar than the Elmore James tune. People love to see a woman wailing on a blues axe. There's something primordially sexy about it. Killer shredded it. LaTonya broke a stick. Without missing a beat she took another one from a cup holder full of them that she'd stuck on her snare stand. Nancy S. turned to give LaTonya shit about breaking the stick and kept up that heavy bass bottom that made the blues song enter your heart with a thump. These girls were bad!

But sometimes too much of a good thing can be too much of a good thing. The band was provocative to a certain a type of man. The girls didn't mean to incite. It wasn't their fault. It was the men, their lack of control, their immaturity, the beer. It didn't happen often, but this night one of the patrons got too drunk and started to paw LaTonya during a break.

"Hey, brown sugar. Come on over here and sit on my lap." He tried to pull her toward him when she left the stage.

"F%$# off, dude." LaTonya shoved him away. She didn't take this kind of crap from anybody. But the guy had lost his sense of—his sense of anything, really. He thought he was being cool. He was middle-aged, skinny but with a pot belly from the beer, a grey ponytail, and dressed in shiny leathers that gave him away as a wannabe weekend rider.

"Come on, Honey."

"I'm not your honey!"

A heavily muscled, bald dude in a Harley jacket with a ZZ Top beard and sunglasses rumbled out of the crowd and intervened on LaTonya's behalf.

"This little f%$#er bothering you?"

"Not a 'tall," said LaTonya. She could take care of herself, especially against any drunk fool. But the Mr. Billy Gibbons lookalike wasn't just being a Good Samaritan. He wanted to beat on somebody righteously. The Quaffery usually had such a gentle vibe, but now was oozing tension like a leaky crankcase. LaTonya stepped in between the stupid drunk and the biker, turned her back on the Harley dude and spoke to the intoxicated man in a quiet voice. "Git on out of here before my friend messes up your ugly face."

That was the foolish fellow's exit cue, and he should have walked away, but he just didn't know what he was doing. Being drunk explains a lot, excuses a lot, but reaching out to try to tweak LaTonya's nipples crossed the line. Nan raised the shoulder strap of her bass over her head and brought the instrument around as if she was going to whack him with it, baseball bat style. As she started her backswing the Harley guy grabbed it so fast he spun her around—

"—Don't damage your axe, girl. He ain't worth it." Without another word he stepped forward and smashed the guy in the face. He went down, staggered to his feet, and was overwhelmed by a half-dozen guys in matching club jackets who beat and stomped him for about ten seconds until LaTonya shrieked—

"—Don't kill him. Don't kill the drunk fool!" Somebody must've called the cops already, because they were there in about a minute. The injured man was carted away by ambulance. Nobody was arrested. Everybody started drinking their beers again. The Blues Girls resumed their set. The next year The Blues Girls had a Billboard Hot 100 hit song the three of them had co-written called *Don't Kill the Drunk Fool Blues* that was streamed by a large crossover audience. They went from playing places like the Quabbin Quaffery to opening for big name acts on tour. They were on their way, thanks to that drunk fool.

Deerfield: A Train Robbery

William Armes was descended from a long line of Armes who had been in the Pioneer Valley since before the American Revolution. His father, Richard Armes, had worked for the railroad for many years, and was an occasional drinker at the Caboose during its brief run as a guerilla bar. Richard's machine shop, housed in an old red barn on River Road along the Connecticut River in Deerfield, was almost a museum of iron-working. It contained immense machines salvaged from the railroad yard—lathes and grinders and benders and metal presses, along with preposterously huge wrenches, hammers, and other tools required for working on the locomotives and train cars that passed through the East

Deerfield rail yard. Richard used the machines and tools now to make custom parts for tractors and other heavy machinery. The son, William, thought of a different use.

William had a little drug problem—he was a heroin addict. It had started as for so many others with a sports injury—he'd been the star halfback on the Frontier football team until he tore a knee ligament in his senior year. The doctor gave him oxycodone, which led him to oxycontin, which led him to heroin. Failed drug tests made it hard for him to hold a full-time job. His father Richard was disgusted but sympathetic. William could look at his father and see exactly what he himself would look like in thirty years, if he lived that long. Both were tall, beak-nosed men with full heads of hair, Richard's now pure white, William's still glossy black. Richard had kept his physique from the years of arduous rail yard work, and still got up every morning at 5:30 a.m. to feed and milk the family's small dairy herd. William was already letting his once athletic body go soft. Richard didn't kick William out of the house, and allowed him to use the machine shop for odd jobs. But repairing bicycles and lawn mowers wasn't going to get it done for William, who needed increasing amounts of ready cash to support his habit. He came up with a crazy plan to become a train robber like Jesse James and Butch Cassidy. He enlisted the help of a couple of junkie buddies, Jimmy Wise (left tackle on the high school football team) and Charley Woods (defensive back). Together they planned a caper they thought would bring them notoriety as well as cash for more dope.

It started, like many train robberies in the Old West, with a derailment. Contrary to the myth portrayed in movie Westerns, cowboys like "Baconrind Bill" didn't leap from their horse onto moving trains. They either bought a ticket and waited for an opportune moment, or they derailed the train and attacked in the ensuing chaos. The trains that passed through the East Deerfield rail yard were all freighters, so buying a ticket was out of the question. With his father's tools, William figured a derailment would be easy. But what could they rob in a long train of coal cars, pressurized tankers, and open cars heaped with construction material rubbish headed for the biomass plant out in Pittsfield? They needed inside information on some valuable but small cargo they could take and sell for easy money. That part was easy. William's girlfriend Melissa (also a junkie) was a secretary in the railroad office. She told William that the most valuable cargo the trains in this area carried was that of the railroad itself. An old car that had once functioned as the private car of a wealthy robber baron had a safe in it that had never been removed. Even though the car was now just a caboose and all the fancy furnishings had been stripped out of it, the railroad transported its local payroll in the safe. It was a matter of expediency, and a quaint nod to nostalgia. They never figured that would include an attempt at a train robbery. Melissa, an attractive blonde girl and former Frontier cheerleader, should never have gotten mixed up with William. But it was inevitable; they'd been childhood sweethearts before the descent into heroin madness. The promise of more of that sweet soporific was all it took for Melissa to provide

William with a schedule of when the train with the caboose holding the safe would be in the rail yard.

Some of the trains that come through the East Deerfield rail yard are so long that crews have to back them over the rail bridge across the Connecticut River into Montague to turn them around or shunt them onto different tracks. That was where William thought he could pull off his theft. The rail bridge was less than a mile from his father's home on River Road in Deerfield. He figured he could derail the train, rip open the safe, take the cash, and be home in bed before the police even arrived.

The plan, such as it was, was for William and Jimmy to hop onto the train with homemade explosives, cause a derailment while the end of the train was in Montague, and then run back over the bridge with the loot, jump into the getaway car where Charley was supposed to be waiting in the rail yard, and take off while the police raced to the scene of the crime across the river.

Ah, but in the words of the Scottish poet:

The best laid schemes o' Mice an' Men
Gang aft agley
An' lea'e us nought but grief an' pain
For promis'd joy

The train was late, some two hours late, which was enough time for his supposed accomplices Jimmy and Charley to shoot up twice more and doze off and miss the thing all together. That left William out there on the bridge alone, without a helper to bust open the safe and without a getaway car to get away in. Oh, the car was parked in the rail yard parking lot all right, but Jimmy and Charley were asleep in it, leaning against each other like two doughy little boys whose mother had left them in the car while she shopped.

Worse, the train wasn't long enough to reach the other side of the river. The caboose containing the safe was stopped on the trestle over the icy waters while the engineer was doing some minor maintenance work on the locomotive. That was good for William's plan to cause a derailment, but bad for positioning. He'd thought he'd be in Montague. William wasn't sure what would happen if he tried to derail the train while it was on the trestle. The whole long line of cars, which included tankers carrying who knew what kind of hazardous materials, might crash into the waters below, taking him with it. But William was an addict, and even when not under the influence of opioids was not a person known for his great decision-making—hence the whole ludicrous robbery idea in the first place. His thought process went along the lines of *"Well, what the hell, if it goes it goes, it's been a shit life anyway, and if it works I'll have all this cash for dope and I won't be sharing with those assholes Jimmy and Charley, just with Mel."* The thought crossed his mind that with the train stuck on the bridge he didn't need to cause a derailment. He could just blow the safe. But the thought didn't stick. He went with the plan. He used the oversized wrench he'd brought along to loosen the coupling, set an explosive charge on the second to last car, practically hanging off the bridge to do it, watching the malevolent river flow beneath his feet through the gaps between the railroad ties. He ran some ignition wires back onto the third to last car and paused just for a minute as if common sense and self-preservation were about to kick in, then yelled *"F$#k it!"* out loud and pushed the button on the crude timer he'd rigged up. There was a flash and a severe rocking of the train, and for an instant William thought he'd brought down the whole trestle. Then the last car, the one containing the safe, separated at the front coupling and plunged into the icy Connecticut, almost dragging the locomotive and all the other cars with it. The heavy engine stayed on the tracks and kept all the cars behind it perched precariously off their rails but still on the trestle, saving the lives of the train engineer and his assistant, who immediately initiated emergency procedures that included an automated call to the local and state police. The locomotive engine was in the rail yard while the last car was on the bridge. *That's not what was supposed to f#@$kin' happen*, William thought, dazed and shaken by the catastrophe that had just occurred.

A train derailment can be a federal case, depending on what falls off, for example, if dangerous chemicals leaked from a tank car. In this case it was just the old luxury car turned caboose with the company safe on it that had taken the plunge, but the engineer didn't know that. The caboose was a half mile and sixty cars back. He just knew his computerized display panel was flashing an unscheduled decoupling. The engineer threw the emergency brake to lock the stopped train in place. His assistant leaped from the locomotive and began to run back toward the end of the train.

Meanwhile William was recovering from the shock of seeing the caboose disappear into the dark swirling waters below. He realized he was now stuck on the end of a derailed train that wasn't going anywhere. If he scooted forward along the train he'd have to confront the engineer, Tom Vogel, a friend of his father whom William had known since childhood. If he ran away from the train into Montague he might be able to get away before the cops came, but he'd be stuck without a car and would have to walk home over the old rail bridge that had been turned into a bike path. That would bring him into the rail yard where the police would be sure to be gathered. Still that seemed like the better option. He knew already that Jimmy and Charley wouldn't keep their mouths shut. When the police woke them out of their drug-induced slumber, they'd name him as the ringleader, which he was. William saw no way out of his predicament, and briefly thought of just letting himself drop into the river, where the frigid waters would bear him away and under for good. But he was too much of a coward for that. He scuttled along the trestle until he reached the place where the bridge met solid ground in Montague, and fled into the night. He decided to walk the long way around, down into Sunderland and across the blue Sunderland Bridge and back up River Road to home, hoping to evade the police that way, but it was no use. The cops had River Road blocked off at Keith Cross Road. After a brief desultory attempt at hiding in the woods, William came out at the first bark of the K-9 dog.

Richard Armes came to the police station in South Deerfield at midnight to bail out William. Before the cell door opened that stared at each other through the bars for a moment.

"Sorry, Dad."

"We gotta get you some treatment, son." They walked out of the station at around 3:00 a.m. and were back in bed before the sun came up, just like William had planned.

The boys, William, Jimmy, and Charley, got the notoriety they craved, though not the cash. In addition, Jimmy and Charley each got two years in Walpole. William got five. Melissa got off with probation and stint in mandatory rehab that changed her life. Years later, a happily married suburban housewife, she'd tell her story as it if it had happened to someone else. She'd show visitors clippings from the *Greenfield Recorder*—mug shots of her and the boys, the derailed train caught in the stark relief of night floodlights, the caboose in the shallows with one end buried in gravel and the other end sticking up, wheels exposed like a shameless hussy.

"We were young then, and wild," she'd say with more than a trace of pride. Plastic surgery had removed the shooting-up scars from the inside crooks of her elbows.

William discovered mindful meditation in prison, and emerged a transformed person who never touched drugs or alcohol again. He joined a nearby Zen center, became a monk, and devoted his life to helping other incarcerated men to find stability and meaning in their lives.

Ashfield: Meet the Fine Sisters

It was the morning of the Ashfield Fall Festival. Columbus Day weekend. Barbara Fine and her sister Ellen were having breakfast at Elmer's Store. Originally built as a general store in 1835, Elmer's has seen a great many changes over the years, yet it remains essentially the same both inside and out. How can both these things be true? It's easy. The slogan on the Elmer's website says it all: ***The Kind of Place That Isn't There Anymore – Except Here.*** The Ashfield Fall Festival is what town fairs used to be like. There's a home-made catapult held together with duct tape that launches pumpkins toward a cardboard castle held together with duct tape. Old Farmer Brown (that really is his name) leads his team of champion oxen down Main Street. Local fiddlers play. A few modest food stands offer local baked goods and hot spiced cider. There are booths with local crafts. Ceramic, woolen, wooden, whatnot. Ellen and Barbara Fine had lived in Ashfield for more than 80 years. They'd been having coffee and scones at Elmer's since the late 1990s when it changed from being a grocery store to more of a café. They were going to have the same today.

Ellen and Barbara looked like twins, but they weren't—Ellen was a year older. They dressed like twins though, usually in the same outfits right down to hats and gloves. A few years ago, the current owner of Elmer's had playfully put a brass plaque above the tiny table near the front where they sat: "The Fine Table." There they sat now, grey hair in buns, hats and gloves on the bench beside them; trim elders, not from formal exercise like many of their "active senior" peers, but from strict adherence to a strict New England diet: fish on Friday, root vegetables in winter, apples in apple season, corn in corn season. And they walked every day, rain, snow, or shine, from their home on the outskirts of town to their table at Elmer's. They were both short and high-waisted, which gave them a pixie look. As the people of Ashfield knew, you didn't want to cross them. They liked propriety, and looked down from DAR heights on anyone who lacked it. This particular morning they were out early because they didn't plan to attend the Ashfield Fall Festival--"too many people," Barbara sniffed--and they wanted to get their morning coffee in before the crowds gathered, and then walk back to their grand old tattered mansion, a stately Victorian badly in need of a paint job, with cracked windows and a debatable roof, and inside, crammed with relics of an earlier era. It was furnished with old-fashioned easy chairs with antimacassar doilies, a cherry-wood roll-up desk, rotary phones, that sort of thing. But it was neat, not a hoarder's house, on Main Street at the very edge of town. They were planning to settle in and shut the door for the rest of the weekend. The fair hadn't started, and the tourists hadn't arrived, when there was a commotion on Main Street. The two sisters peered out the window as a group of about twenty black people passed in a straggling procession, followed by a few town kids.

The local church had sponsored a refugee family from Somalia. There'd been lots of support in town for the project, and the First Congregational Church on Main Street had raised almost $20,000 for the project. Now the families made their first appearance, walking down Main Street, the women in full hijab, the men bearded and tense. A few local children followed behind, intensely curious. Kids can be cruel anywhere, in big cities or in small towns like Ashfield. These kids weren't being mean, but they were being a little rude by tagging along so closely, and one of them uttered what might have been a timid taunt.

"My, my," Ellen said. "I thought it would be a man and his wife and some kids, you know, a family. This is a whole group."

"Indeed."

"Still, those boys ought to be respectful."

"Agreed." They looked at each other, these two prim and proper New England spinsters, and then they rose as one and walked outside.

"You there, boys! Stop that!" For such a diminutive woman, Ellen's voice thundered like a coach at a ball game. People up and down the street turned to see what was going on.

The boys ran away without uttering another sound. They knew who the Fine Sisters were and the consequences of defying them. Barbara Fine approached the eldest man in the group, a very tall thin man dressed in all white with a white knitted skullcap.

"Coffee?" she said.

"Thank you, but they are expecting us in church." The man spoke English perfectly, with a formal British accent.

"Those kids won't bother you again. I'll be calling their parents later. They'll reprimand the boys, and you'll receive an apology from them in person directly."

"That's not necessary."

"Oh, yes. It is necessary. We must maintain decorum here in Ashfield."

"Thank you." The man turned to go. The little group waited until he was in the lead again and then fell in behind him. The Church was just down the street and across the road from Elmer's. The two sisters watched them in silence. When they were out of hearing range, Barbara said to Ellen:

"That went well, didn't it?"

When they went back inside to finish their coffee and pastries, they were greeted by a round of applause from the morning breakfasters. There was a happy buzz in the café. It was fall. Vibrant autumn leaves were turning Main Street into a blaze of glory, the Festival was starting at noon. The Fine sisters had made a welcoming gesture to the new refugee families. And, lest you think that something terrible happened later on that day, let me put your mind at ease. Sam Denson, who had won the skillet-throwing contest (Men's Division) down in Conway, put on an exhibition with Jane Hebert who had won the Women's Division. The Pumpkingames went off without a hitch, though the Festival had to put out a last-minute call for more zucchini to use as bowling pins. The Antique Car parade had a few new entries. There was Morris dancing, the aforementioned fiddling, a couple of bagpipers, lots of money raised for the Ashfield Citizens' Scholarship Fund. Like the sign on Elmer's Store says, Ashfield is the kind of place that isn't there anymore – except here. Sure, there are opioid problems in Ashfield, just like in most small towns in Western Massachusetts and the rest of New England. It's an epidemic. Unemployment is high, the town hall needs a new boiler, couples get divorced at the going rate, and all the other daily problems of life exist here as commonly as in the big cities. But the kids still do 4H; most of them even go to college. No one can remember the last murder in Ashfield. Life moves at a slower, more measured pace than elsewhere. As long as the very fine Fine sisters continue to hold court at Elmer's Store in the mornings, Ashfield remains a sanctuary of the world.

Springfield: A Turners Falls Cop in Springfield

Springfield 3 Mi. ← Rt. 20 → Worcester → Boston →
35 Mi. 90 Mi.

Trase's Tourist Court
339 Boston Road "The Finest in New England"

ii

As far as Daniel Masters was concerned, being a small-town police officer was about the best job he could imagine. There were a few meth heads and heroin addicts who lived in the old millworkers' brick row houses along Avenue A, and a few bad apples out on "the island," that spit of land between the canal and the Connecticut River riverbed, but it wasn't much. A knifing or two (non-lethal) on the weekend. A few domestic disturbances, a bar brawl at Jack's Tavern. Mostly he got to ride around in a shiny new cruiser, write a few speeding tickets, and pull construction duty for a few extra bucks of overtime. If Daniel envied his sister Carla for being on a larger force in a bigger city down in Springfield, he didn't show it. These local dope addicts were strictly minor league compared to what he'd seen as a Marine in Afghanistan.

Nobody was burying IEDs on Main Street in Turners. He was happy to lead the low-key life of a small-town cop. He was helping his community and he was largely keeping the demons from his Marine days at bay. If a guy and his old lady got into it, you put them in separate cells for a couple hours, or send the woman to her parents for the night. If a guy tore up a bar, you threw him in jail until he paid the damages or at least promised to. But what the hell do you do when a creep is stalking your sister? Daniel was the older brother. He and Carla might not be all that close as adults. But this was personal. Ever since she'd called to confide in him what was going on, he'd been on edge.

The situation reminded him of Afghanistan after all, where the enemy was all around, there was no battle line, and the only thing that made sense was to be constantly vigilant your whole tour, never let your guard down for even a second, and that was exhausting, nobody could do it, and as soon as you let go, BAM! Something bad happened.

He drove down to Springfield to meet with Carla, taking his own truck, a big old American diesel brute, not the cruiser. Technically, this wasn't police business. He had no jurisdiction. He didn't wear his uniform, but he did carry his badge and his gun.

He met Carla at an Irish bar on Main Street. It was a dark place that poured Guinness draft and gave out bowls of peanuts whose discarded shells littered the floor. They took a booth in the back. Once they'd settled in and ordered, he started to ask her about the shit that was going down. It was awkward on several levels. They were brother and sister. She outranked him. But he was older and he'd been in the war and seen things.

"Seems like you're attracting the wrong kind of guy," Dan said.

"Aw, Petras isn't so bad—"

"—Come on, sis. I got a look at his rap sheet. He's a very bad boy."

They both leaned back at the same time and spread their arms out, and caught each other's amusement at seeing the sibling parallelism of their movements.

"Good to see you, sis."

"You too, bro."

"Your boyfriend—"

"—Ex."

"Your ex-boyfriend, he needs to stay away from you."

"Yeah, I guess so. He scared my roommate." The half-dozen screens that were carrying the Sox game erupted in synchronous noise when the burly Dominican slugger who DH'ed for the Sox hit one over the left-field light stanchion onto Lansdowne Street. In the bar hardly anybody lifted their head.

"I could do something. Unofficially, I mean."

"Like what?"

"You know. Find his motel room, confront him a little—"

"—'Confront him a little?'"

"Yeah. The direct approach. 'Stay away from my sister.' Bullies like him, they don't like that."

"You can't do that, Dan. First off, it's dangerous. Second, you don't have any authority down here, as you know—"

It got messy, old family stuff mixing with the present ugly situation. Finally Dan gave up talking with Carla and got up and left. But he didn't give up on the idea. It only took him a half-hour to find Petras Fotopoulos registered under his own name in a cheap motel room at the edge of Springfield.

It was one of those motels where you can pull your car right up in front of your room. Noisy air conditioning, thin sheets, fuzzy cable TV, pressboard furniture. Dan parked his truck a block or so away, and walked back to the motel. Daniel Masters pounded on Petras' door at 10:00 p.m. that evening. No answer. He pounded again, this time with his flashlight, which he had brought along as a second weapon. Nothing. But instinct told him that Petras was in there.

"Hey, buddy, come on out and talk to me."

Nothing. Dan decided to put his cards on the table.

"Petras Fotopoulos. I wanna talk to you."

A faint stirring, or maybe just a sharp reflexive intake of breath. The guy obviously didn't like it that Dan knew his name. The door opened as far as flimsy antiquated chain lock would allow. Petras peered out through the crack.

"Who the f%$k are you?" Petras asked, though it was clear from first glance that Petras had sized up Dan as a police officer. "What the f%$k do you want? And show me a badge while you're at it."

Dan stepped back a foot so that the scene wasn't quite as confrontational.

"I don't have a badge. I just wanna talk to you."

"No badge? F%$k off."

"Stay away from my sister."

Petras broke into an ugly laugh. "Shoulda f%$kin' known. It's like a little family up here. Everybody knows everybody. Cozy. And now I know you."

"Stay away from Carla."

"Are you a Springfield cop?"

"No."

"Are you even a cop? You look like one."

"Turners Falls."

"Where the f%$k is that?"

"Up river."

"Up river. That ain't a direction, that's a--I don't know what the f%$k it is. I'm going to come 'up river' and visit you."

"Looking forward to that."

"Asshole."

"Punk."

"Hold on a second."

Petras opened the door, and stuck his chest into Dan's chest. "Beat it, pal."

Neither of them wanted to fight in the motel parking lot, but something had to happen-- They closed on each other as if they were shaking hands and grappled silently, upright, almost like they were old buddies sharing a hug, but there was a viciousness to it that any bystander would have seen. Petras showed a knife but didn't use it, and Dan had one hand on his flashlight but resisted the opportunity to crown Petras with it. After a few seconds, they separated. They were both sweating in the humid August heat. Dan was by far the bigger man, but at close quarters he recognized a dangerous enemy in

Petras. The knife was just a bluff, he knew the thug wouldn't use it here; he was too exposed.

"Stay away from my sister."

"F%$k off."

Dan smiled, a mean little smile, and said: "Listen f$#@ker, I did two tours in Afghanistan. The Taliban make guys like you look like pussies."

"Get f%$king lost or I'll call the cops on you for impersonating."

It was an empty threat, but it ended the confrontation. Petras went back inside, but Dan could sense he was still watching through the flimsy curtains of the motel room. He'd be gone in the morning, if not tonight. *That really went well*, Dan thought wryly. He turned to backtrack to his truck. He wondered how he'd explain this to Carla, who'd warned him not to come. He didn't have anything to prove to this low-life; he was just another punk as far as Dan was concerned. *I'd like to see this guy take on six Afghani Taliban stoned on hash and carrying Kalashnikovs and RPGs*, Dan thought as he reached his truck. He took a quick look around in case Petras had followed him, but that hadn't happened. The more he thought about it, the more he thought he'd done the right thing. Why hadn't Carla asked anybody on the SPD for help? They should have her back. Maybe it was because she was the first woman to make rank. That was Carla. Nothing stopped her, she was a force of nature. He pulled away from the curb and took side streets up to 91 North and the way home.

Brookfield: Town Meeting Night

There is no better place to witness the characters of the Pioneer Valley in action than at town meeting. These meetings are held in small towns all over the valley. Let's drop in on the Brookfield town meeting. Brookfield Town Hall is a stately old brick building with a clock tower, and a large open Great Hall on the second floor. Built in 1904, the whole place has been recently refurbished. The wood floors gleam and light flows in from the magnificently arched windows. Well before the 7:00 p.m. meeting start time, the hall starts to fill up with the wonderfully various assortment of characters who make up the citizenry of Brookfield.

The characters portrayed in this story are fictional. None of them live in Brookfield. They are representatives of the valley as a whole. Treat them with kindness. Love them. They are the tart but delicious mature fruit of a crabby old tree that has been growing since the Revolution.

Take Adam Peabody, for instance. From those Peabodys, after whom a town in Eastern Massachusetts is named. Right up there with the Cabots and the Lodges at one time. Adam is a descendant of settlers who were given tracts of land in the Pioneer Valley, then thought of as "The West." They could own the land if they homesteaded for five years consecutively. Few could. Many turned back, or were driven out by the Wampanoags, the Pocumtucks, Nipmucs, or other tribes. Those that stayed were the hardy ones, the tough ones. the ones who could fight off the Indians, cull their fields of stones, and grow crops in the unforgiving earth. If the blood has gotten a little diluted over the years, and if these modern Peabodys aren't as physically fit as their forebearers, trust that they are still of the strongly rigid Puritan mindset. Change doesn't come easily to them. They continue to use tractors that became obsolete thirty years ago. They bale their hay in rectangles, not in cylinders. You get the idea. Adam is one of those men. Six feet three inches tall and patricianly straight. Shock of white hair. Slightly beady black eyes. And that curious Western Massachusetts accent, very mild, not nearly the broad A of Boston, but still there like an embossed stamp of history on the tongue. In Town Meeting, Adam Peabody is the guy who always gets up to speak and the guy no one wants to see get up and speak. They've all heard his rant many times. They know it will be long, and boring, and most of the time everybody else is on the other side of whatever issue he speaks about. But Brookfield's is an open town meeting, run loosely on Robert's *Rules of Order* for parliamentary procedure. Any registered voter can vote and is allowed to speak on any topic. So, not five minutes into the meeting, there he is, rising from the fourth row on the right where he always sits, and making his way toward the podium. The Town Manager and moderator of the meeting, John Darslewski was expecting him. Adam and John are old friends. They've known each other since grade school. John's the town's lawyer, as well as being involved in its politics. Adam's a sixth-generation farmer. They come from different cultures and live in different worlds, yet at Town Meeting they are like old comrades at arms. John's job is to keep Adam from taking over the meeting. Adam's job is to make his point, however long that takes. But it's not about Robert's Rules, it's more like two old friends jawing about the Sox starting pitching. The meeting hall is small enough that everyone can hear everything that is said without microphones, but there are mikes and video for the local cable TV broadcast, so when Adam says to John:

"I just want to weigh in on the purchase of the fire truck, John," everyone hears John's response, and everything that follows.

"That's Article 6, Adam." John is looking up from five foot seven at the stately Adam. John's roly-poly round and presents a jovial face, but he's nobody's fool. By virtue of his profession he knows everybody's business, and is widely trusted with managing estates, and handling real estate transactions.

"Well, I'm up here now, you're not going to make me make walk back and up here again, are ya? My knees aren't in it."

The lawyerly Darslewski makes a motion to allow Adam Peabody to speak about Article Six out of turn. The motion is passed by the three-member Board of Selectmen sitting to the left of the moderator. The main function of the Board, comprised of two men and one woman all of whom are long-time residents of the town, is to hinder the actions and effectiveness of the town manager. But before John cedes the podium to Adam, he turns to the audience and gives them the old Thoreau chestnut that they've heard almost as frequently as Adam Peabody's diatribes:

"Adam here puts me in mind of Henry David Thoreau, who said: *'When, in some obscure country town, the farmers come together to a special town-meeting, to express their opinion on some subject which is vexing the land, that, I think, is the true Congress, and the most respectable one that is ever assembled in the United States.'* We're not all farmers anymore, but Adam here is, so let's give him his due."

John steps aside and sits down. Adam adjusts the mike upward, and looks out over the assembled crowd. He nods to a few acquaintances—Mrs. Velma Freeman, the white-haired lady in the front row, handbag in her lap, hat on her head the like of which has not been seen on Broadway in a century. Always chipper, always supportive of the speakers, no matter which side of a debate they advocated, Velma is especially fond of Adam, who is a widower and she being a widow. Sitting beside her is her son Sam Freeman. Sam is a chubby, pasty-faced, reclusive loner who plays video games all day by himself. But he comes to Town Meeting faithfully with his mother, driving her in a vintage Cadillac he keeps in pristine condition in the wooden garage attached to their house by a mudroom. Town politics is Velma's main entertainment. She watches all the town meetings on local community cable television, Planning, Zoning, even the Conservation Committee, and comes to them in person when she can. Sometimes you'll still see old crones like Velma on a New England back road, drawing water from a well or raking in their garden, women who are often relegated to assisted living or nursing homes, but with fiercely independent spirit have hung on and maintained their own homes, long after their husbands passed. Except for the driving, it's Velma who takes care of Sam, not the other way around. She cooks his dinner, does his laundry, pays the bills. Sam's claim to fame is a few thousand virtual points in some obscure Japanese video game.

Glaring at Adam from across the aisle in the second row is William Willard, another old Pioneer Valley family name, whose forebears go as far back as the Peabodys. Like that family, the Willards were from another town to the east that had sent hardy pioneers to brave the wilderness. Willard wants the town to have a new fire truck. Adam thinks the vintage machines the town owns now suffice. A few yuppie types have moved into town, making it more of a commute town to Worcester or even Boston than ever before. These newcomers talk fiscal responsibility but also want the best schools for their kids. They are ambivalent about a new fire truck—they don't want the town to spend money unnecessarily, but they don't want their houses to burn down because of obsolete equipment either. Many of them are uncomfortable already because there is no real fire department, only a bunch of volunteers. Undependable. Not that they would ever volunteer to join.

"Can we get on with it already?" Willard whines after Adam Peabody has nodded and acknowledged a half dozen audience members. Adam smiles at Willard

"What's your hurry, William? The meeting's only just started." A low groan rises from the audience. "But okay, let me outline my opposition to spending money on a new fire truck." Adam begins a lengthy recitation of the history of the Brookfield Volunteer Fire Department, enumerating his many relatives who had served in its ranks, and briefly launching into a description of the first brass hand-pumper that had served the community for well over 60 years in the 19th century, before an exasperated John Darslewski finally brings him back into the 21st century.

"Adam, focus, please. We have twenty-three articles to get through by the end of the evening, and you've skipped to Article Six. We're going to have to go back and start over when you've finished. So please, make your points now. Please."

"My point, dear John, is that the current fire truck doesn't need to be replaced. It's still working perfectly—" This last point is immediately challenged by the current chief, Bob Worsley, who is seated in the audience but feels he has to say something—

"—It's costing us five thou a year to maintain, Adam."

"My point exactly, Bob," Adam says and smiles insouciantly. "At five thousand dollars a year you could keep the current truck for another sixty years—"

"—Oh, this is too much," William Willard shouts. Voices are heard from both sides of the argument, for there are people in the hall who agree with Adam Peabody even if they don't want to hear him speak any more.

"Order, order!" town manager and moderator John yells. It takes a moment for the noise to subside. "Listen, people this shouldn't be that complicated. Either we vote to spend the money for a new truck, or not. It's not rocket science. I suggest we skip all further debate and go right to a vote on Article Six. Then we can circle back on Article One, which is simply to accept last year's annual report—"

"—Or not," says Adam, but by this time John Darslewski has gently moved Adam aside and taken over the main microphone—"

"—All in favor of an immediate vote on Article Six, please raise your hands—" It's nearly unanimous. "All right then. All in favor of funding the purchase of a new fire truck for the Brookfield Volunteer Fire Department, at a cost of $357,433, to be amortized over the next twenty-five years, raise your hands." This vote is closer, requiring the Town Clerk, Kathy Majewski, to walk the hall and make a careful count before informing John Darslewski of the results. "The vote is 117 in favor, 96 opposed. Article Six is carried."

Adam Peabody looks like he wants to say a few more words but thinks better of it and shuffles back to his seat. You might think that would be the end of Article Six, but after the town has worked its way through the first five articles, mostly administrative and pro forma items, Article Six rears its ugly head again.

"What kind of fire truck are you going to buy?" a voice calls out from the assembled. Moderator John can't see who spoke. Selectman Roger Warren raises his hand. He's on the Finance Committee and in charge of Purchasing for the town. He's got an accountant's looks— black rectangular glasses, butch cut grey hair, cleanshaven, wearing crisp dress pants and a button-down shirt. He's come prepared. He reads from a paper he holds in his right hand:

"It's a SL75 aerial ladder quint. Monarch cab and chassis; Cummins ISL 450-hp engine; Hale Qmax 2,000-gpm pump; UPF Poly 500-gallon tank; 304 stainless steel body; aluminum huck-bolted 75-foot aerial; Smart Power 10-kW generator; Command Light LED light tower; Akron Brass electric monitor."

"See, that's what I'm talking about," Adam rises and shouts from his seat in the audience. "Why do we need all that truck? We only have but one or two fires a year."

"I'm sorry, Adam, but we're on to Article Seven," says John Darslewski, but that doesn't stifle Adam.

"And by the by, aside from the mechanics among us, did anybody understand that technical gobbledy-gook?" Here Adam should have known better, because there were a good number of men in Brookfield, mostly the farmers, who did understand about large engines, and they began debating amongst themselves in the hall, ignoring Darslewski's mountingly irritated calls for "Order!" Finally giving up, John Darslewski sits down and opens up the battered and beloved copy of his favorite book: *History of North Brookfield, Massachusetts. Preceded by an account of old Quabaug, Indian and English occupation, 1647-1676; Brookfield records, 1686-1783*, a tome that he carries with him everywhere. And therein he read this comforting passage, that soothes his troubled mind, while around him the debate rages over the particulars of the already passed Article Six:

"The first celebration of Independence in Brookfield was held July 4, 1784. The following account of the affair was given by Eben T. F. Newell, then 9 years old, who was present: *'The celebration was held on West Brookfield plain. An Ox, neatly dressed, and perfectly roasted, with hoofs and horns on, was sliced, and the pieces laid on tables, with piles of bread, and plenty of rum and water. The people passed in order between the tables, each taking bread and beef in their hands, and helping themselves to the rum and water. Scipio Witt, a colored man, who had served in the army, bored holes in 13 large chestnut logs, loaded and primed them, and so fixed the slow matches that a regular salute of 13 reports was heard by the people on the plain, who were taken completely by surprise. We children were greatly pleased to hear the noise, and see the fragments of broken logs fly up in wild confusion.'*"[xiv]

Pittsfield: Growing Up in Pittsfield

Back then, everybody worked at "The G.E." as they called it. Everybody had a job. After work every night they'd head over to the Madison Bar and drink away their wages. Get up the next day and do it again. Their kids had that to look forward to—or so they thought. Time and change proved otherwise. But then growing up in Pittsfield was idyllic. There were still woods and horse pastures within the city limits, and landmarks the kids had named themselves: Slippery Rock, Spooky Trail. There were tough neighborhoods the kids didn't go, where the older kids there would kidnap them for a few hours, and they couldn't tell whether it was in fun or for real. And there was Joey, Matt and Steve. They played

together every day over the summer, went to the same
Catholic elementary, junior high, and high schools
together. They all played the same three sports: Football
in the fall, hockey (not basketball) in the winter, and
baseball in the spring. That's just the way it was. Joey
was the catcher, stocky, strong, stubborn, opinionated.
Matt was the introspective one, shy around girls, tall and
not quite fitting into his body yet. Steve was Mr. All-Star
everything, the best athlete of the bunch, blonde and
handsome, who could skate backwards faster than most
kids could skate forwards. It was 1961, but it still felt like
the Fifties, even though there was a young, energetic new
president and the winds of change were rustling the air.

They made fun of the campers who came to Camp
Allegro for girls or Camp Onota for boys over the
summer. They'd hide out in the woods and scare the crap
out of the girls by pretending to be madmen in the
woods. Along about age sixteen they started drinking
heavily and taking up with the girls seriously. Of course,
it was Matt, the timid one, who ended up getting Marion
Thompson, one of the Allegro girls, pregnant that
summer. What a mess! They ran away, and hid in a
cabin in the woods that they thought only they knew
about, but Marion's father, a foreman at The G.E.,
rounded up some of his work crew and they went into the
woods with flashlights and found them and brought
Marion home. Later they heard she went off somewhere
to have the baby. She wouldn't recover her reputation
until she went off to college. Matt was heart-broken. All it
did was make him drink more. And that was enough to

change the world for a lot of people in Pittsfield that summer.

They couldn't drink in the bars their fathers drank in because the drinking age was 21 and the oldest of the three of them was 17. But Joey had an older brother who would buy for them. They'd scrape together enough money for a case o' 'Gansett or Genny creme ale (because they were near the New York border, where the drinking age was 18), and take it out in the woods. Once they got good and plastered they'd drive back into town and see what trouble they could get into. It wasn't hard. Sometimes they'd drive in circles around the round barn at the Shaker Village, until they got chased off. Or in the summer they'd go to the high school and play drunken basketball (until they got chased off). Mostly, though, they'd just drive up and down the streets of the city, showing off Steve's T-Bird, with its chrome thunderbird logo on the rear beneath the covered keyhole, and its angular fins and round taillights like tits. Yeah, it was regular *American Graffiti* stuff. Only sometimes the American dream gets lost in something darker. It was like Silver Lake. On the surface it looked like a lovely body of water, but The G.E. had been dumping stuff in there for years. One time the police found a car in the lake that had gone off the road. There was a dead body inside. When the tow truck dragged the car out of the water, the cops thought must be an old wreck because the body was so badly decomposed. But it turned out the car had crashed only the week before, and whatever The G.E. had been putting into the lake had caused the body to rot quickly. Nobody swam in Silver Lake much after that.

One night Joey's brother brought them a bottle of whiskey instead of the usual case of beer. The beer was a self-regulating mechanism—one could only drink so much of it without pissing it away, and the drunk one got from it was bouncy and light. The whiskey had no such restraint. They got viciously drunk and quickly. The three boys staggered around in the woods until Matt announced he was going to cruise by Marion Thompson's house. Matt had been pining to see her all summer. Marion's father had warned him to stay away. The whiskey gave him the false courage to go. Steve and Joey joined him. They took Steve's T-Bird and left the other two cars in the woods. All the way into town they were shouting and singing and swerving all over the road, but they didn't care, they were young, they were strong, they were immortal. First, they just drove by silently. The house was shuttered up, and they didn't know if anyone was home. The second pass Matt honked the T-Bird's horn, but got no response. The third time they slowed down and Matt jumped out while the car was still moving forward. He rolled on the ground was nearly run over by a car going the other way that blared its horn at him. Matt stood up and gave the other driver the finger. Then he walked unsteadily up to the porch and banged on the front door.

"Marion! Come on out here. It's the father of your child!"

Matt sounded sincere and lost. Steve and Joey howled with laughter. The door opened and there stood Mr. Thompson, arms crossed, biceps bulging, a look of malignity on his ruddy face. He was an ex-Marine who'd been in the Korean War. He was fiercely protective of his daughter.

"Get the hell off my porch or I'll go get my birding gun and blow your brains out, which I should have done when you—" but he couldn't bring himself to say 'got my daughter pregnant'.

Fueled by the whiskey, Matt stood his ground. "Is she here?"

"No, she ain't here, and even if she was you couldn't see her. I told you, get off my property or you're going to have a load of birdshot up your ass, or worse!"

"Where is she?"

"None of your goddamned business," Mr. Thompson said through gritted teeth.

"Is she having the baby?"

"Of course she's having—listen, I'm going to count to three and then I'm—" but he didn't even start to count, he just slammed the door shut.

"Come on, Matt, let's go!" Steve yelled.

Matt teetered uncertainly, caught between his desire to see Marion and the threat of being shot. Steve and Joey weren't so conflicted. Steve revved the T-Bird engine and leaned on his horn. Joey could see that Matt was frozen. He leaped out of the car and ran to the porch and dragged Matt off it, just in time, because Mr. Thompson appeared again, with his 12-gauge, and no doubt he'd have used it, if the boys hadn't roared off with a screeching of tires that brought other neighbors out to see what the commotion was all about. The T-Bird careened around the corner at the end of the street, fishtailed, straightened out, and picked up speed. It wasn't clear who was driving. It was Steve's car, but sometimes Joey liked to "hot rod it" as he called it. They went tearing down West Street. Joey lost control. They smashed into a tree. One boy flew through the windshield. They all died. The next day rubberneckers drove by all day. The wreck was lodged against the tree, the exaggerated tailfins pointed downward like a missile that had failed and smashed into the ground. The car was so mangled that it was difficult to tell who'd been driving. The only easy identification was the one, Matt, who'd been in the back seat, and had been launched through the front windshield.

At the funerals (the three boys were buried together) Matt's father and Mr. Thompson got into a fight and the police had to be called. For everybody else, life went on. The Fifties feeling finally turned into the true Sixties. Pittsfield started a long downward slide, driven by a series of closings at The G.E. factory that had once employed 13,000 people. Eventually the plant shut down all together, leaving only the PCBs (polychlorinated biphenyls) it had dumped into the Housatonic River, and a clean-up that continues to this day.

Westfield: The Whip City Bar and Factory

Just across the river and a block up Elm Street from the old Westfield Whip Manufacturing Company factory was Whip City Brew, a pub variously described in online reviews as "a comfortable place," and "like Baghdad, depleted and bombed out." Nobody agreed on the quality of the food or the beer either. It was a very popular place. Whip City Brew was where Patrick McCole sat, nursing an IPA and wondering if his luck was going to change. If it was, Whip City Brew was an unlikely place for it to happen. The employees of Westfield Whip Manufacturing Company, of which Patrick McCole was one, were some of the most loyal patrons of Whip City Brew, and Patrick was there a lot.

The nickname "Whip City," came from when the town was the nation's number one manufacturer of buggy whips. The bottom dropped out of that market precipitously when automobiles came in. One of the last remnants of that industry was the Westfield Whip Manufacturing Company, the last whip manufacturer still in operation in Westfield. It still manufactured whips and sold them all over the world.

Patrick McCole just wanted to finish his Accounting degree at Westfield State up the road. Instead he found himself working ten-hour shifts in a nineteenth-century factory making products he had thought no one had any use for in this twenty-first century. It was hard to combine long day shifts with night school classes. Patrick felt like his life was slipping away. He was a couple years older than most of his classmates because he'd had to take a couple years working to save enough to start school. He noticed the difference in class between himself and the slightly younger, more traditional college kids, coming straight from high school and some who had not even worked summer jobs. That was okay. Patrick was determined to be successful. If he didn't get arrested first. Damn! What had he got himself into?

It had started as a favor to the father of one of his Whip City Mfg. Co. co-employees. Seemed harmless enough. Use his burgeoning accounting skills to help a small business owner catch up on badly out of date books. Pick up a few bucks on the side. What could be wrong with that?

He met the employee's father's friend, Rico Pastronelli, at the fancy La Fiorentina bakery down in the

South End of Springfield. Rico wanted to meet him at a
bakery instead of at his home where he ran his small
business. Patrick had been to the South End many times
for food before the casino came in. Now he mostly
avoided it. On a Tuesday evening he drove up from
Westfield to Springfield and sat at a table in La Fiorentina, surrounded by the rich desserts: huge, heavily
frosted cakes, many kinds of cookies, rich, ricotta-stuffed
cannoli. The sweetly strong licorice smell of anis hung in
the air. Patrick ordered a Napoleon and sat at a table, not
sure how he would recognize his new employer. Ten
minutes later a man came in wearing the kind of
greatcoat you don't see much anymore in this age of
down jackets. It was full-length, tweed, and very heavy. It
encased a very large man who passed right by Patrick W.
without looking at him and went to the counter, where he
was greeted like an old friend and handed an enormous
pink box without waiting. Only after he had paid and
made small talk with the little old Italian grandmother
type at the register did he turn and acknowledge Patrick.
He sat down without being asked and stuck out a large
paw.

"Rico Pastronelli."

"Mr. Pastronelli."

"Rico, please. You are Patrick McCole?"

"Yes."

"Thanks for coming, Patrick. I tell you, it's not easy to
find somebody who understands this accounting stuff.
You'd think it would be, but it isn't. I heard you're doing
really well over there at State."

"Thank you."

"And you want to make a little extra to cover the shortfall between scholarships and tuition?"

"Yes, sir. I appreciate the opportunity."

"Okay, well, listen, I have the same problem as you. A little shortfall. Only my problem can be solved much more easily than yours. All I need is a little fuzzy accounting, not serious double-bookkeeping, you understand, just a couple slightly off back dates."

Back dates? Patrick thought, while he sat across from this large man with a florid nose and narrow eyes boring into him. *Hell, it was such common practice that some people didn't even think it was breaking the law.*

"I think I can help you," he said simply.

"I thought so." Rico reached into the voluminous coat and pulled out a substantial sheaf of papers. He tossed them onto the table casually.

"Here they are."

Patrick was startled. "I mean, I can't do them here, right now. I have to read them at least."

"No problem. How about we meet again here in a week? Does a thousand sound fair?"

"Extremely generous, thank you." A thousand dollars! With what he'd saved already, that extra thousand would get him through spring semester!

Patrick took home the papers and perused them. Even after reading them it was a slight mystery exactly what business Rico Pastronelli was in, but all that was required of Patrick was to fill in a few dates with entries earlier than the actual dates. Patrick's mother was a real estate agent. He knew that house closing forms were backdated all the time to get deals done. He imagined the same to be true here. It was just a technicality. He didn't feel bad about it, except for one tiny little detail. There was a place on the form where he had to sign acknowledging *"the veracity of all the information contained therein."* Was he ready to do that? He wasn't an accountant yet, just a student of accountancy. But these forms didn't need to be signed off by a full-fledged accountant, just by a third-party—him. All well and good. He read the documents, signed the forms, sent them to an address Rico had provided, and a week later, received a check for a thousand dollars that he deposited immediately into his student loan line of credit. And that was that.

Except it wasn't. The next week Rico asked him for a few more back-datings, plus signing someone else's signature on a couple mysterious Requests for Transfer. Even this, signing for someone else, Patrick could say in a stretch was not uncommon in his mother's real estate business. But a week later Rico asked him to 'cook the books' with a little of that aforementioned double-bookkeeping, which he hadn't done yet. Now Patrick knew he was in too deep. It felt like hell, or at least purgatory, a place you go and there's no clear idea when you're going to get out. He couldn't go to the police; that would be like signing his own confession. He tried to make himself scarce, unavailable to Rico, which is why he could be found after work this day at Whip City Brew, a place he assumed Rico, with his spotless greatcoat and shiny black shoes, would never frequent.

At the bar, Patrick chatted with Caitlin, one of the pretty bartenders. There were two of them, Caitlin and

Meaghan. Both were blondes. Both wore nearly thigh-high black boots over jeans, an odd choice, he thought, for standing on your feet all day.

"F#$ing Whip City."

"You mean the factory or this place?" Caitlin asked.

"I mean the whole town. Sucky nickname, too."

"Hey, lots of the towns in the Pioneer Valley have nicknames—Holyoke—'Paper City'."

Patrick was ready to play. "Gardner—'Chair City'."

"Chicopee—'Kielbasa Capitol of the World'." The female bartender snorted a laugh.

"Greenfield—'Gateway to the Berkshires', even though the Berkshires are nowhere in sight. Nicknames like Paper City and Chair City don't fit anymore because the mills are gone," Patrick said morosely. "But, lucky me, we've still got Westfield Whip Manufacturing Company." He was too tired to include an obscenity. Caitlin brought him another IPA unbidden.

"So, Caitlin, what would you do if somebody asked you to do something illegal—?"

"—Happens all the time—"

"—No, but I mean, asks you to do something illegal and then ups the ante, you know, asks you to do something *really* illegal, and threatens you if you don't do it?"

"I'd want to know the details."

Yeah, right. So would I, Patrick thought, but to Caitlin he merely said, "I'm in deep shit." Caitlin gave him a sympathetic glance but just then was called away by another guy down the bar. *Jesus, what am I going to do?* He could move to Florida or Arizona or somewhere and start over, but that would mean giving up his college aspirations. No way he could move and afford to keep going to school. The one thing he couldn't do was tell Rico he didn't want to work for him anymore. So, what was he going to do? He had no clue. Patrick looked around Whip City Brew at the scuffed dance floor, the ancient pool tables, the neon beer ads and posters that had been there forever. If he couldn't finish college, he might end up working here with Caitlin and Meaghan, taking out bottles and trash, sweeping the floor, washing dishes in the kitchen. He could see no way out of his predicament. The prospect was almost more than he could bear. He drank two more beers in rapid succession, went back to his tiny one-bedroom apartment and fell asleep early.

And then, just as Patrick McCole was thinking about the worst of possibilities, the problem solved itself. The next morning the front page of the *Springfield Republican* covered in lurid detail the murder of Rico Pastronelli, gunned down on the streets of the South End of Springfield in classic mob fashion. He was found still clutching a pink box of cannoli from La Fiorentina. On reading the news, Patrick immediately shredded and threw away anything he had that was associated with Rico Pastronelli. Fortunately, he hadn't started the double-bookkeeping yet. The police called Patrick in to ask about his name on the back-dated documents, and he told them the truth, that he'd been asked to do a favor by a college friend, and he'd done it. He didn't mention the forgeries. After all, it wasn't his name on those documents, and he didn't see how they could track those back to him. The police never followed up with him on those items or anything else. Patrick never mentioned what he'd done to anyone, ever. Three days after the murder, another check for a thousand dollars arrived in Patrick's mailbox. He deposited it.

Patrick graduated from Westfield State with honors and a degree in Accounting. Later he put himself through law school and is now a highly respected lawyer in Springfield, known for his honesty and integrity.

West Springfield: The Circus at the Big E

Aerial View of Eastern States Exposition Grounds, Springfield, Mass. 68365

v

Peter Bishop learned how to juggle and ride a unicycle in junior high school. He entertained his friends with pratfalls and funny little routines. He was a born athlete, with the lithe, flexible body of a gymnast and the long sad face of a clown, and nowhere to use his skills and natural gifts except as the class clown, or in boring little school productions. But there are hardly any clowns anymore. They've fallen out of favor. When people think of clowns today they mostly imagine the "creepy clown with a knife" meme from videos on the internet.

Every year Peter's family would go all together to the Big E, West Springfield's annual extravaganza of dog shows, horse shows, a poultry congress, 4H displays and competitions, car shows, motorcycle shows, a railroad hobby event, woodworking, firearms and other crafts.

Some members of his family went mostly for the bizarre food concoctions—fried beer, fried butter, deep-fried cannoli, potatoes from Idaho the size of loaves of bread, burgers made from kangaroo, camel, and alligator meat. Peter went for the circuses. Some years the shows were disappointing, with tame animal acts like midget ponies, especially after the circuses stopped using elephants. Some years they were thrilling—Russian acrobats doing amazing tricks on high-wires and trapeze swings.

Peter usually found the clowns unsatisfying. They played the comedy broadly, going for the lowest common denominator, which made the six-year-olds in the audience happy. He'd never seen Cirque du Soleil or the Big Apple Circus but Peter had an idea that circuses could be much more than what he saw at the Big E. Still, he loved the excitement and the old-fashioned carny quality of the shows. There was usually a ringmaster in tails and top-hat, with a couple of glamorous female assistants in tight-fitting sequined gowns. The whole Big E had a sweet old-fashioned feel to it, that made Peter think he could still somehow succeed at his secret dream of performing under the Big Top.

This year, Peter's senior year in high school, when he was supposed to be choosing a college, the Big E circus was a small-time troupe from the Midwest. They were a rough-looking bunch. Most of the performers were East European refugees and the crew were hardcore carny characters with muscles, tattoos, and greasy black hair, probably Roma, gypsies. This rag-tag troupe was presided over by a snarling, arrogant, imperious impresario whose name was Magnus the Magnificent. In the hours before the first show was to occur, Magnus could be seen directing the setup of the ring to his precise specifications. They had to be precise because the pony on whose back the young lady from the Czech Republic rode was very particular about the circumference of the ring and had been known to refuse to perform if those dimensions were not exactly to its liking. Peter took in the show with wide eyes, admiring the grace and skill of the pony rider, who performed elaborate and dangerous gymnastic tricks, leaping on and off the horse repeatedly as it trotted briskly around. He was frustrated as usual by the clowns who opened for the pony and rider act. They seemed bored and weren't doing much to hide it, and Peter thought he was a better juggler than either of the two who passed flaming torches between them while a third clown pretended to be frightened as he ran back and forth underneath the fiery clubs. Afterwards he hung around while his family went off to gorge themselves on the weird food offerings. While Magnus was directing the re-set of the props for the next show, he noticed Peter loitering nearby and called him over. Peter practically ran in his excitement, and stood nervously with his hands behind his back as Magnus the Magnificent addressed him.

"Like the show, kid?"

"Oh yeah, it was great!"

"Sir." Magnus preferred to be called "Sir," and he let Peter know right away, with a stern look.

"It was great, sir."

"Wanna meet the Princess?"

"You mean the girl who—"

"She's no girl, but yes."

"I'd love to. Sir."

"Wait here."

Magnus disappeared behind the bleacher seats that had been set up around the ring, and came back in a couple minutes with 'the princess,' who turned out to be an almost middle-aged woman, whose face was smeared with garish streaks because she was halfway through taking off the heavy make-up that made her appear like an ingenue, from a distance.

"Hi," said Peter. The princess said nothing.

"Come on Stepanka, be nice, the boy is a fan."

"I love your tricks," Peter mumbled shyly. "And the pony."

"Thank you." The heavy Czech accent made it sound like she was angry, but it was just the way she talked. After an awkward moment Stepanka looked at Magnus, who dismissed her with a curt nod.

"Don't mind her, she's tired after her performance."

"She's beautiful."

"Ya think so?"

"Oh, yes! Yessir."

"Ya wanna run away and join the circus, kid?"

"Maybe. Yeah. I can juggle, and ride a unicycle."

"Don't get ahead of yourself. You like mud?"

"Huh?"

"Most of our shows are outside, and we get a lot of rain. Hence, mud."

"I'm okay with it."

"You 18?"

"Yes, sir."

"Okay. Here's the deal. Ya get $117 a week and a place to sleep on the train. We'd start you off mucking the animals' stalls and helping with the setup and breakdown of the show. No performing until ya pay your dues, understand?"

"Yeah. Yes, sir."

"If ya wanna join us, be at the Springfield train station at midnight tonight."

"Okay."

Magnus the Magnificent turned and went about his business and Peter trailed out of the arena and went to look for his family. He knew he shouldn't do it, couldn't do it. He was too young to give himself permission. He had lied about his age. He wouldn't be eighteen for another seven months, but he suspected the impresario didn't care. He knew his family would never allow it, and once they found him and brought him back he'd lose all privileges for like forever. Still, it was so romantic to think about traveling around America, sleeping on a train. Maybe he'd even date the gymnast on the pony. He was such a dreamer! For the rest of the day he wandered around the Big E in a daze, and when the family piled into the car to go home, his mother asked him if he was feeling okay. Peter took this as an opportunity to set up the circumstances for an escape.

"My stomach's a little off. Guess I shouldn't have eaten those deep-fried Twinkies," he said. When they got home he went straight to his room and secretly began to pack a small backpack. He stuffed his juggling balls into it, even though the impresario had told him he wouldn't be doing any performing at least for a while. A couple pairs of jeans, a few shirts, socks, and underwear. His copy of a favorite circus history book. An extra pair of shoes because of the mud. That was pretty much it. Around 10:30 p.m. he snuck out of the house, a modest ranch in the suburbs on the outskirts of West Springfield, walked a mile down to the local strip mall and called a cab. By 11:30 p.m. he was in Springfield. He asked the lady at the all-night ticket counter and was told that the circus train was on a siding and that he couldn't go there without permission. He left and snuck his way across the tracks until he located the train, which was just a few shabby cars and an old locomotive idling on a stem of the main line. A roughneck came out to shoo him away but Peter held his ground and mentioned Magnus's name.

"All right, wait here," he was told. It was a warm night, a nearly full moon lighting the sky along with the lights of downtown Springfield, suffusing the area around the train with a magical white glow. It felt a little dangerous to be here, with big machinery all around him. Peter was following his dream and wasn't going to think about his parents and his siblings asleep in their cozy house in West Springfield. He was on an adventure!

The next morning Peter's parents discovered to their horror that Peter was gone. He'd left a note saying not to worry about him, that he'd gotten a job and wasn't going to finish high school. It didn't take a genius to figure out what had happened, and by mid-morning Peter's father was in a car headed for the Bedford County Fairgrounds just south of Altoona, Pennsylvania, the next stop in the circus's itinerary.

Meanwhile, Peter had passed an eventful night and morning. He'd never seen Magnus the Magnificent, but he'd been led to a bunk on the train by a midget named Billy who was part of the clown contingent. Peter had taken Amtrak to the City a few times, but he'd never slept on a train and as the machine rumbled south, stopping frequently, Peter was too excited to sleep and from his upper bunk he stared out a narrow horizontal window at the passing scenery, lit by the moon and lights along the track. He was homesick already, and feeling like he should have left more of a note for his family. Yesterday seemed like a lifetime ago. He was just dozing off when Billy came back around. It was dawn. Peter staggered out of his bed, still in his clothes from last night, and followed Billy through the crowded car where everybody else was still sleeping and onto the fairgrounds. Sometime in the night the animals had been led from the train into stalls in a big old tin shed that was nothing like the red wooden barns he was familiar with in New England. Blinking in the dawn light, he stumbled into the shed and was handed a shovel.

"Muck 'em and brush 'em," Billy said gruffly.

"When is breakfast?" Peter asked, because he was realizing he hadn't had anything to eat since those godawful Twinkies yesterday afternoon.

"Work first, then eat," he was told. It soon became clear to him that he wasn't going to be spending any time with Magnus the Magnificent or with the pony princess gymnast either. He was a common laborer, the lowest of the low. He was given the job no one else wanted to do, mucking the train car stalls. Well, that's what Magnus had told him, he shouldn't be surprised. Peter had grown up in suburbia. He had no experience with animals, and got kicked pretty good by the prima donna pony that was the star of the show, and knew it. Once he wandered outside just to get a look at where he was, somewhere in southern Pennsylvania, he'd been told, but Billy was right there shooing him back into the shed. It began to dawn on Peter than this was what his life was going to be like for the foreseeable future, and that he might have made a colossal mistake. He went back in and finished his chores, and Billy led him to the dining car, which was a misnomer, it was just a bare interior with picnic tables nailed into the flooring. The food was downright miserable, powdered eggs, nasty sausages, and cold burnt toast. But Peter was hungry and ate his fill before being sent out to help with the construction of the trapeze for the afternoon matinee. He caught a glimpse of the Czech gymnast practicing for the show, but she ignored him. He never spoke to her aside from that first introduction at the Big E.

Peter's father arrived at four in the afternoon, tired, hungry, and angry. He'd driven straight through, stopping only for gas. He sought out Magnus and confronted him before even looking for Peter. Magnus wasn't hard to find. The matinee had just finished, and he was still in his imposing ringleader's costume, tails and top-hat. He was unperturbed by the angry parent. This wasn't the first time a starry-eyed teen had joined his troupe, and it wasn't the first time a father had arrived to take him back.

"I could have charges brought against you for corrupting a minor," Peter's father shouted in Magnus's face. But Magnus the Magnificent was having none of it.

"Hey, the kid told us he was eighteen. We're a circus. We don't check IDs."

"Where is he?"

"He's with the animals, where all the kids start out."

"Well, go get him."

"Already done."

Sure enough, here came Peter, looking exhausted and bedraggled, and relieved. He ran up and gave his father a big hug before he could get too mad at him.

"Let's go, son."

"I have to get my backpack." But that had been arranged for also—Billy came around the corner holding it.

"Bye, Billy," said Peter.

"Bye, kid. Come back when you're old enough."

"The hell he will," Peter's father said, and turned and marched toward the parking lot, Peter trailing behind him.

Later in life, when he had become a businessman like his father, he only juggled to entertain his children and their friends at birthdays and pool parties. Every year he would take his children to the Big E and with a hint of wistful regret he would tell them about the day he had run away with the circus.

Old Deerfield: Reenactment of the Raid of 1704

We thought we were safe. We thought they could not get inside the palisade. Who among us could have predicted a snowfall so heavy that wind-blown snow banks would make a walkway to the top of our precious stockade? Had we but known we would have taken further precautions. But what could we have done? There were so few of us. The heathens were so savage, the cowardly French so cruel and deceitful.

I was reading an account of the attack to a group of schoolchildren. I couldn't tell it the way it really happened, with the bloody massacre, the violent killing of infants and stragglers. The school administration would have my head. But I wanted to make it come to life for my class of seventh-graders. I wanted to make them feel history. It was February, the same month as the February 29th, 1704 raid. I decided I would take them on a field trip they would never forget. Because of planetary

warming, none of the kids in my class had ever seen the
Connecticut River freeze over hard enough to walk on it.
In fact, none of their parents had either. You had to go
back many years to the last time that happened, though
not all the way back to 1704. There was no way for me to
have them out there on that modestly wide beautiful
river, laboring upstream in a blizzard. But we could
simulate the experience. We started at one of the old
houses on Main Street in Old Deerfield. We enlisted the
help of the Pocumtuck Valley Memorial Association, the
local historical society, not associated with Historic
Deerfield that owned most of the houses and the
museum along the street, the two organizations
maintaining a New England matronly, cordial, proprie-
tary reserve with each other. PVMA supplied us with
period dress for the colonials. Historic Deerfield let us
into the Ashley house two hours before dawn.

The part the kids weren't expecting was that I had
hired a group of local Native Americans. I had done so
with the full support of the school administration who
thought it would be "culturally educational." The Native
Americans would play the parts of the raiding Indians. I
met with them once, and they seemed like a nice enough
group, a bunch of farmers and blue-collar workers and a
scattering of professionals. Family men, most of them.
They were proud of their heritage and dedicated to
preserving Native American history. They'd had some
success in changing the local historic markers to remove
references to "savages" and "massacres." They all
attended the pow-wow every August up in the Deerfield
River valley out by Charlemont. They understood these

were middle-schoolers they were playing for, and they didn't plan anything violent or scary, just some whooping and a little shoving along the retreat route, to give it an air of realism. Several parents insisted on coming along as chaperones. I encouraged that for the sake of transparency. I asked them to dress up in colonial clothes too. A local videographer was supposed to tape the whole thing, but thank god she canceled at the last minute. We all, the kids and the parents, left our cell phones and other devices behind at the start of the exercise for the sake of realism. The unanticipated benefit of this was that there was no record of what happened next.

The raid went off without a hitch. We watched as the "Indians" climbed over a nearby fence that was a stand-in for the stockade, and came crashing into the Ashley house, screaming and howling horribly and waving axes and hatchets, and herded us all outside.

We started walking through the cornfield to the north of Historic Deerfield, following the route the original raiders took to get back to the Connecticut—around the left of Pine Hill and down into the Deerfield River bottom. It was bitterly cold, and very quickly it became apparent that the rough woolens supplied by PVMA were not the fleece and goose down and temperature-resistant synthetics these kids were used to wearing in winter. These Eaglebrook kids are the sons of the super-rich. They have their own ski slope with its own chair lift, and there's a Charles Schwab swimming pool. They aren't used to much of any roughing it, unless you count a cold day on the slopes at Aspen. I tell them to look back. The

"Indians" along with a few Native Americans dressed as French disguising themselves as Indians, are "burning" part of the town, here represented by a few bales of hay in front of one of the historic homes, under the watchful eyes of the Deerfield Volunteer Fire Department. It's a mirage, but the crackling flames add to the effect as the kids are being rushed away from the village and into the field. Some of them stumble in the corn stubble and a parent glares at me. One of the "Indian" actors makes wild gestures to us that we are going to the river. Up ahead is my stand-in for the Connecticut, the smaller Deerfield River, also not frozen over but unlike the Connecticut River, accessible along its banks. The route of the raiders in 1704 must have taken them this way. We would pass through the corn-stubbled fields, then under Route 5, and hug along the edge of the Deerfield up to its confluence with the Connecticut River. The meeting of the two rivers is a historic spot where for hundreds of years Native American tribes gathered under truce to fish in peace, until 1676, some 28 years before the Deerfield raid, when the colonials under Captain William Turner massacred the village of Peskeompscut in a surprise attack during King Phillip's War, a war that also included the Battle of Bloody Brook in Deerfield. Buses were waiting in the rail yard parking lot to bring the kids back to Eaglebrook for a hot lunch. It had all sounded so simple, so innocent, so instructive and educational.

"These are the descendants of the Abenaki and Caughnawaga tribes," I told the kids. "They're now represented by the Wampanoag tribe."

"Why?" some smart-alec in the class asked. I was going to respond but one of the Native American actors, overhearing my attempt to explain, cut me off sharply—

—"Because the State of Massachusetts wanted to lump us all together, even as far back as 1742— Mashpee, Peqout, Nimuc, Pocumtuck, hell, they would've thrown the Mohawks in there too. But we're not like that. We each have our own cultures and customs. Just in this area in addition to the Pocumtuck, there were, Nonotucks, Quaboags, Woronocos, Agawams—you there!—" he yelled at me "—Get back in line. We kill the weak ones who fall behind."

"That's cruel!" one of the kids yells.

"No! It's smart. Because we're going to be marching more than 300 miles up the Connecticut, Wells and Winooski Rivers, through Vermont and into Quebec. Losers don't make it." His use of the word "Losers" made some of the kids laugh. The actor raised his war club, a blunt, nasty-looking piece of hickory with a hefty curling knob on one end, and shook it in one boy's face.

"You want your brains splattered on this field?"

"Hey, hey!" I rushed over and told the actor sotto voce to cool it, that his language and attitude were too real. He shrugged and laughed maliciously, but backed off.

Soon after, one of the Eaglebrook parent chaperones came up to me. He was a short, heavy man who was unprepared for a hike of this length, in this weather, in these colonial clothes. His hair was in disarray, and his face red from exertion.

"What the hell is going on? This was supposed to be a field trip. It's turning into a forced march!"

"The boys can handle it. Half of them are on the hockey team I coach. They're used to this weather," I said.

"You'd better hope nothing happens to them, or you'll be out of a job, pronto." He fell back, unable to keep pace with me as we trudged on, passing under Route 5 at the bridge where at least three previous bridges including two rail bridges had once crossed the Deerfield. The group huddled together for warmth and was walking along the edge of the river where some ice had formed. I had to warn them not to venture out on it. The shore was rocky, uneven, and sometimes steep, but it was safe, and there was a crude trail. I didn't know if it was an animal trail or one used by the kayakers and canoeists for portage, but I'd scouted it out with the guy from the Native American group a few days previous and it had seemed okay. Now, though, with thirty middle-schoolers and half-dozen sullen and suspicious parents in tow, I was less sure this had been a good idea for a path to the rendezvous point. We could climb out of the declivity and walk the rest of the way on River Road to the rail yard, but I didn't want to do that, it would spoil the adventure and break the realism of the arduous struggle that the settlers had endured. So, we pushed on, in our own small way attempting to mimic the truly horrific trials the captives of 1704 endured. And then up ahead a scuffle broke out—one of the Native American actors was beating a kid, not with a club thank god but with his open hand. I rushed up and pulled him off the kid.

"What the hell is this?!" I cried.

"Little bitch stole a feather from me. Sacred feather. Come down from my ancestors. Give it back, bitch!" By this time the whole outing was about to become my worst nightmare. Kids and parents were crowding around, everybody was shouting at me. I used my best teacher voice:

"Everybody, back off! Dylan—" I addressed the kid accused of theft, a trouble-maker, classic spoiled rich kid who thought he was entitled to anything and everything he could get his hands on. Now he was playing the part of victim, sniveling and pointing a finger at the actor who had stepped back a couple paces to let me mediate—"Did you take this man's feather?"

"It's right there in his hand!" the now relaxed actor said, his outrage muted and dignified.

And so it was. I managed to calm the situation. Thankfully Dylan's parents weren't among the chaperones. Later I had to defend myself in front of a lynch mob called the Eaglebrook Parent-Teachers Conference. Fortunately the kids were on my side--they all said how much they enjoyed the hike, even Dylan. After a contentious meeting it was decided that I had done nothing wrong.

A few months after the event, during summer vacation I drove up to Charlemont. It was the day before the annual pow-wow. I talked with a small group that included most of the of the actors from my disastrous historical recreation. We met in a pizza parlor in town, not at the Indian Shop farther back toward Greenfield on the Mohawk Trail. I sprang for the pies. I asked them what their experience of the event had been.

"Those little rich f%$kers," a middle-aged man who was not the one I'd met when I negotiated the group's participation. I didn't know who this guy was, sitting across from me in a diner booth, wearing blue jeans and cowboy boots and a cowboy hat, black hair in a ponytail, face weathered like granite, but he wasn't an outsider. The other guys all knew him. "You're lucky Slow Runnin' Jimmie didn't cut that friggin' kid's head off. Then you would have had a real reenactment."

"I'm sorry, but I don't know you, and I don't remember seeing you there."

"They call me Wandering Bull. I wasn't there. I don't participate in those things. Not that there's anything wrong with it, especially the ones like that one where the Indians win!" He smiled at me. Why didn't it feel like it was a smile?

"I guess that's true. Some of the captives became involved with their captors and stayed and became part of tribes and wouldn't come back," I said. There was a rustle at the table. They'd heard this one before. My new cowboy friend called me out:

"Nah. You got your facts wrong there, Teach. We didn't turn them into Indians. We sold them to the French and they turned them into Roman Catholics, which was worse in the eyes of those settlers!"

Everybody at the table laughed, including me. And suddenly I felt like it was all going to be all right. I wasn't going to lose my job. I'd made history more real than they would have experienced it otherwise. Later one kid wrote in his yearbook that it was the highlight of his time at school. And these guys I was having pizza with, the

Native Americans who had played their parts a little too well, they were becoming my friends. I had more in common with them than with the progeny of the elite down in Old Deerfield. The hike, field trip, re-creation, whatever you want to call it, had transformed me more than it had the kids. I had a new appreciation of the struggles of the Native Americans.

Wandering Bull studied me coldly. "I'm going to give you a quote," he said, "to take back to those boys. This is from the storyteller Dovie Thompson of the Kiowa Apache tribe: 'Americans are strangers we invited for dinner 500 years ago that are still here.' Can you hear that? Can you hear me?" he asked.

"I hear you," I said, and I did. We clinked bottles and toasted each other silently.

Chesterfield: A Mystery in the Gorge

The Chesterfield Gorge has been called the Grand Canyon of Massachusetts. Unlike the Grand Canyon with its staggering grandeur, the Gorge is a pleasant, steep-sided ravine, a nice place for a short day-hike. The East Branch of the Westfield River runs through it. But as Sheila Lebeaux found out one winter day, in the words of astrophysicist Arthur Stanley Eddington: "*Not only is the universe stranger than we imagine, it is stranger than we can imagine.*"

Sheila was a hiker. Every weekend, regardless of the season, if she was home at her cabin on Ireland Street she would walk to the trailhead and hike the short half-mile trail to the gorge. It was a strange hobby for the sturdy, single, grey-haired, middle-aged woman, who spent her weekdays as animal control officer for towns in the western Pioneer Valley, often trekking miles in the woods in search of wounded animals, and enforcing hunting license laws. But she found joy in the solitude and beauty of nature, and enjoyed it more than she could express. This January day she had the lovely gorge to herself. There were no footprints in the snow as she hiked down the precipitous trail from the parking lot at the head of the chasm. Sheila was wearing snowshoes because she enjoyed the feeling of moving across the top of the crust instead of sinking in. With a practiced gait she made the hike that followed the river and gradually descended down to where the rapids plunging down through the sheer-sided canyon leveled out and the water ran more calmly and smoothly.

As she neared the river Sheila saw a strange phenomenon from a distance. Half a dozen people were out there, in the dead of winter, building cairns. You've seen those little stone towers in streams near your house, that people create when no one is looking, to delight and mystify children and others easily entertained. Sheila had noticed these cairns out along the river's edge before, and she didn't like them. For her the natural beauty of the place was enough, and the piles of rocks were intrusions, manmade arrangements that were out of place in the wild. She never tampered with them. Let people have their fun was her thought. But where had these cairn builders come from today? There was only one path down into the gorge. And something was not quite right. The perspective seemed all wrong. The people appeared to be only slightly larger than the cairns! And they were dressed queerly, in hooded brown robes with thick white rope belts, like monks. She blinked and rubbed her eyes, trying to reconcile her frame of reference. As she watched, startled and amazed, she saw that it took two of them to lift a small rock that she could have picked up easily. What was going on? It didn't make sense to her senses.

"Hey!" she shouted. One of the robed figures looked up at her and smiled. He had the face of an old leprechaun, pinched and wizened. It was so queer she shook her head to clear it, and when she looked again, they were gone! Breaking into a run, which was not easy to do in snowshoes, she dashed down the last bit of trail to the river. When she got to the place where the cairns stood, she observed tiny footprints in the snow around them, smaller even than impressions a child's foot would make.

"Hey!" she yelled again, looking around wildly, but her voice was met with silence. Strangely, she wasn't afraid, just intensely curious. She felt an odd sort of calm. What had she witnessed? It was like a dream. She had no explanation for it. She tromped along the bed of the gorge, trying to follow the diminutive footmarks, but they petered out and were lost on the ice along the edge of the river. She hadn't brought a phone or camera, and it was starting to snow, which would soon obliterate the tracks. After a while she gave up and turned back. She walked home slowly, made herself a cup of tea and pondered what she had seen. It would remain forever a mystery to her, an enigma that she could not explain away. She never told anyone of her experience, fearing they would think she was crazy. She continued to visit the gorge almost every weekend, but never saw the robed elfin figures again. Every once in a while over the years, she would think back on that winter day, and wonder just what she had witnessed.

Arthur Stanley Eddington also said this: "*Something unknown is doing we don't know what.*"

Eastfield: The Imaginary Town

Eastfield does not appear on maps of Western Massachusetts. If it were somewhere, it would be in those wilds of the Berkshire hills out by Savoy, Peru, and Florida, down a long, twisting, forested road, into a narrow valley surrounded by high hills. There's only one road in and out. The steep hillsides create a cul-de-sac. It's a place so remote that no outsider goes there, or can even get there. Eastfield doesn't show up on GPS either. One might drive right in and out of it and not even know. The occasional lost traveler who wanders into Eastfield is quickly shunned and urged to leave. Eastfield is a place where everyone lives together in peace and harmony.

Hawley Briggs, the grocer, has an old-fashioned general store in the center of town. He's an important man, everyone gets their groceries from him, with organic veggies and soy and quorn products for the alternative types in Eastfield, and free-range eggs, chickens and beef for everybody else. Hawley wears farmer overalls, plaid shirts, and suspenders, and has a bushy beard. Into Hawley's store comes Molly Eastwick, not an elder but a teacher in the Eastfield Elementary School. She's a beauty, brunette, bosomy, shapely legs. All her boy fifth-graders are in love with her. All the girls want to be like her. Nothing wrong with that. She doesn't buy makeup because she doesn't wear any, and is all the more beautiful for it.

Standing outside Hawley's store is Dwight Bateson, who owns a farm outside of town. He's trying to decide whether he's going to grow corn or cabbage on some upper acres next year, so that he can buy the right kind of seed. Some farmers use oxen, though most have converted to tractors. You'd think Dwight would have figured out what to plant before he got to Hawley's but he was waiting on his intuition to kick in, and so far, it's eluding him. Dwight looks less like a farmer than Hawley does. His hands are dirty from changing the drive-shaft on his classic Farmall Model H row crop tractor this morning. He's not tall, and not all that well-built, but he gets everything done through sheer persistence. Finally, he walks into the store and sees Molly standing there waiting to pay for groceries.

"Hi Molly. My boy Stephen doing well in your class?"

"Hello, Dwight. Yes, he's one of my stars. Of course they all are," she added.

"Of course. So what do you think, Molly, should I grow corn or cabbages next year?" He wasn't really asking her and she knew it, but she played along.

"Gee, Dwight, all I can tell you is the kids like corn at lunch a lot better than cabbage."

"That's good feedback, thanks. You know Mr. Kim would take all the cabbage I grow for his *kim chee* business."

Molly smiled. "I like Mr. Kim's kim chee, in moderation."

"We all do." Mr. Kim was that rarest of creatures, an outsider who had been allowed to stay after he got lost and his car broke down in Eastfield. He had risen from farm day laborer to business owner by plain and simple hard work, a trait the people of Eastfield valued greatly.

Dwight made his decision on the spot. "I'm going to split the difference and plant half of each." Molly, who doesn't know much about farming, nods pleasantly, picks up her purchases and leaves. Hawley and Dwight start up a conversation about the need to keep things natural, with no chemicals or genetically modified seeds. Horses are still used by some for transportation and farming in Eastfield. Everything goes slower with a horse. There are butter churns, and cider presses. No guns other than hunting rifles, no snowmobiles, and no jet skis are allowed in Eastfield. No drones. If you want to get your kicks from noisy smoky, intrusive or violence-producing mechanical devices, you'll have to go elsewhere.

So how can there be any problems in Eastfield? Some young people can't handle living in paradise. They are not content with the idyllic life. They are thinking of leaving. The young have been warned that the outside world is a vast and terrible place. But they are talking amongst themselves about getting out anyway. Eastfield is at a moment of crisis in the town's existence. There's been discussion in the town meeting about whether to open Eastfield to the outside. It's been voted down. Anyone who wants to leave may leave. There's nothing stopping them. But no one has left.

Dwight's older boy, Dennis, a high school senior, not Stephen the fifth-grader, is about to precipitate a critical crisis in the history of Eastfield. He doesn't want to be a farmer like his dad. He wants out. His father is against it. Dennis is having a hard time going against his father's stubborn will. Things come to a head at the dinner table at the Bateson family farm. That evening Mrs. Bateson makes Dennis's favorite meal, chicken with dumplings, baked potatoes, and salad. She knows what is about to happen, simply from maternal intuition. She understands also that there is nothing she can do about it. Not so her husband Dwight, who opens the dinner conversation by saying:

"You won't go. You'll get stuck at the town line, just like the others."

"Others? You mean, other people have tried to leave? Who?"

Mrs. Bateson keeps her head down as her husband Dwight answers.

"Well, me, for instance."

"You, Dad?!"

"Fifty years ago. It was the Sixties, you know. We heard all sorts of things about changes in the world out there, and a few of us decided to find out for ourselves."

"What happened?"

"I told you. We went as far as the town line and turned back. We all realized we were going to be happiest here. You'll find that out too."

"I won't. I'm already gone."

Dennis's younger brother Stephen, the fifth-grader, has been sitting quietly at the table, listening. The brothers are too far apart in age to have been pals, but Stephen worships his older brother. Dennis has already passed down his BB gun, his slingshot, his arrowhead collection, and most of the clothes Stephen wears. Now Stephen bursts into tears and runs from the table. His mother follows after him. Dennis and Dwight sit looking at each other silently. There is nothing more to say.

The next morning Dennis and a half-dozen of his young friends pack up an old truck from the Bateson Farm with their possessions, and head toward the one road out of town in a small convoy, the farm truck in the lead and two cars trailing behind. Dennis drives the truck. He's built like his father, not big but indomitable. Dennis's energy isn't as focused and refined as his father's, but it has a raw power. There's no gate, no barrier to them leaving, nothing but an unseen imaginary psychic barricade in their own minds. They would have to break through it to enter the real world. Dennis pulls up the truck at the town line. There is no signpost. The crossing is delineated only by a change in the color of the

asphalt. He jumps out of the truck and five people get out
of the two following cars—three young men and two
young women. They all stand around as if dazed. None of
them has ever been outside the valley. They are all maybe
a year or two out of high school. If they are ever going to
go, now is the time.

"Are we ready?" Dennis asks the group.

"Why'd you stop? Aren't you ready, Dennis?" Robby
Thompson asks. Robby's an anomaly, he doesn't have
roots in Eastfield, he was adopted somehow by the
Thompson's from a Nigerian family. He is the only
outsider other than Mr. Kim that people could remember
having been accepted in Eastfield, and only because he'd
been an infant when he arrived. The color of his skin has
never been an issue.

"I'm ready," Dennis says. "I just want to make sure
you all are."

"We can always come back, right?" Jane Piskowski
asks. She's afraid. She senses the magnitude of the
change. Usually Jane is one of the brave ones. She was
Salutatorian of her class, varsity singles in tennis, and
dreams of college, which can only be found on the
outside. But now that she stands facing the future so
closely, she is having second thoughts.

"Oh, yes. I asked about that in the town meeting.
They said yes. It's in the minutes."

"I don't know."

"What?"

"You asked if we were ready. I thought I was, now I
don't know."

"C'mon Jane. Your dream, college?"

"I know, but I feel so safe here."

"Feeling safe is overrated," says Dennis. "What we want, the most we can hope for, is to have both. Both the sheltered utopia of Eastfield and the imperfect but dynamic outside world."

"Can we have that?"

"Yes! But only out there. Eastfield is like a security blanket, a place you can always go back to, it's always here."

Someone is crying. It isn't the other young woman, Ava. It's Mike Doucette.

"I gotta go," he says. His black hair is falling in his face and getting wet from his tears. His face is pale.

"Go? Which way?"

"Doesn't matter. I just can't stand here. It's like being on the knife edge. Who's going? Who's staying? Which car should I get in? I gotta move."

Dennis sees that Mike is panicking, and that the whole thing might be falling apart. He does what his dad would have done. Pushing forward, he hops up onto the running board of the truck, and says: "I'm going now. Anybody who's coming with me, follow in whatever car is coming." He jumps in the cab and slams the door, turns on the truck engine, and looks in the rearview mirror. The other five stand there, unable to move. He waits a few seconds, revs the engine, and slowly drives over the line and up the road on a short straightway and then around a bend, until he's gone from sight. The five watch Dennis drive off alone. Each of them wonders silently if they've made the right decision.

"Hey, wait. He's got all our stuff in that truck!" Robby Thompson yells. But none of them start after him. Even the loss of personal possessions can't make them cross that line. They all stay in Eastfield. None of them ever talk about leaving again. Dennis is never heard from. Later on, people in Eastfield talk about the spring that Dennis Bateson disappeared as if no one knew what had happened to him or where he went. People do know, but they choose not to remember, and gradually the memory of Dennis fades. His brother Stephen takes over the family farm from his father Dwight. Life goes on to this day in that forgotten town of Eastfield in that valley to the west, a place beyond recall, existing in a realm where the vagaries of the rest of the world cannot touch it. Call it the Shangri La of the Pioneer Valley. Maybe someday on a drive you'll encounter it by chance. Don't linger there, or you may find that you never want to leave, and maybe they'll let you stay.

Southfield: High School Friends Meet Again

My life and Rick Stetson's went their separate ways after high school, and only came together again one other time, awkwardly. We'd been casual friends growing up in Southfield, which was as we kids liked to say not so cleverly *"the middle of nowhere."* In such a small town, everybody knew everybody. Our town was so insignificant we didn't even have our own high school—most of us took a bus to the local regional high school. The only attraction in Southfield was Campbell Falls, a series of modest waterfalls cascading down the side of a hill off down Norfolk Road. It was a hard place to find. There were two parts of the state park, one in Southfield, one in Norfolk, Connecticut. GPS maps often got it wrong. A trailhead off a small parking lot led to the falls, but as teenagers we hardly left the parking lot, where we drank beer and made out and dreamed of leaving Southfield for somewhere that was somewhere. In high school Rick dated Chloe Farnham, a girl I lusted after hopelessly. Chloe was a farm girl. Her dad worked a hundred acres on a hillside in town, growing corn, cabbage, and hay, mostly. It wasn't the best soil, mostly rocky and unlevel, but he managed to make his living at it. Chloe grew up riding horses, driving the farm tractor, and dancing in school shows. She had long legs and wavy brown hair, a pug nose and wide-set eyes that made her look slightly oriental. It was a look that captivated me, but I was a nobody in the middle of nowhere, a studious geek, while Rick was a three-sports star in high school. It was no contest.

After high school I went off to college and lost track of most of my school friends and acquaintances. Four years passed quickly. I hardly ever came home. I'd gone across the country for college at UCLA and couldn't afford trips back East. In the spring of my senior year I came back for an extended stay after graduation. I was hoping to work and save a little money before I left again for graduate school at University of Illinois at Urbana-Champaign, an engineering university in the Midwest. Southfield felt so small to me after the sprawl and traffic of Los Angeles! But my tiny hometown was also comforting and relaxed. Finding a job wasn't easy though. There were almost no businesses in Southfield, and certainly none that were doing any kind of engineering work. I lucked out when I found a hand-printed index card pinned on a bulletin board in the local coffee shop. Chloe's dad Bill Farnham was hiring seasonal help on his farm. Southfield was so far from everything that Bill couldn't bring in the Mexicans, Guatemalans, or Jamaicans who worked the fields lower down in the valley. He relied on local high school kids. Most of them weren't any good at farm work because they didn't want to do it. It was backbreaking labor, hand-cutting cabbages out of the ground. I called up and put my name in. Bill hired me without even meeting me. He had a crop to bring in.

After my first day I understood why workers were in such short supply. I could hardly straighten up, I was covered in dirt, my clothes were filthy and sweat-soaked, and my knees ached. But I went back the next day and did it again, and after a couple weeks I got stronger and more adept at wielding the knife, and the work got easier. I was hoping to catch a glimpse of Chloe, but she was nowhere in sight. I didn't ask about her. Bill was the strong silent type, not much for small talk. As long as you did your work, he didn't care who you were or what you looked like. I learned from a middle-aged farmhand name Mike that Chloe was still living on the farm. She went off to work in Stockbridge early every morning, cleaning rooms at the big old historic inn there, and came back after dark. That's why I never saw her. But one day we worked late, and I was just climbing into my dad's old pickup when Chloe pulled up in front of the barn. She looked incredibly fetching in her maid's uniform. I waved hesitantly, and she came over.

She put her hand to her forehead theatrically as if trying to remember my name, and then said: "Well if it isn't geeky Bobby Westerland. What are you doing here?"

"Home between college and grad school. Your dad hired me."

"Awesome."

There was an awkward pause. What did we have to say to each other, anyway?

"How's life?" I said, to fill the uncomfortable void.

"No complaints," she said. "I'm saving up money to move to New York."

"New York City?" My shocked response ticked her off.

"Yeah. This girl ain't stayin' on the farm forever. You got a problem with that?"

"No, no, Chloe, I think that's great. What are you going to do there?"

"I'm gonna set up a business to sell organic veggies. I hear those city people will pay big money for high-end produce."

"Great idea," I said. "Has your dad gone organic?"

"No, but I have. Got my own field up behind the barn. I figure I'll drive down every week with the box truck. We're growin' stuff year-round now, in those greenhouses—" she gestured toward opaque white buildings I had scarcely noticed during my time in the cabbage patch.

"Cool. Hey, wanna have dinner sometime?" I blurted out, surprising myself. She astonished me by quickly answering "Yes." I didn't ask about Rick Stetson. I figured in four years they'd either have been married already or the high school romance had ended. Anyway, there'd be time for all that at dinner. I picked her up on Saturday night and we drove into Great Barrington and had dinner at a Mexican restaurant with an unpronounceable name. I impressed her with my Spanish language skills and knowledge of Mexican food. She had Enchiladas Rojas and I had the Pollo Poblano. I didn't tell her that about the only Spanish I knew was how to order Mexican in L.A. We sipped our *agua frescas* appreciatively and talked, shyly at first, but more friendly-like as the evening went on. I knew what my appeal was for Chloe. I was the only one of all our classmates to escape the valley, break out, go off and never come back, until now, and that was only temporary. She wanted to be the next one to make it out, and she wanted me to tell her how I did it. But I had it easy, I had college. She was going to be launching solo, and it wouldn't be easy for her to reach escape velocity. She gave me the quick rundown on some of our mutual acquaintances—

"Suzie Czestochowa's got a hair salon in Southfield. Sonny Telega delivers furniture. Billy O'Connor drives the same school bus he used to ride over to Gateway. No one's left here except you."

I noticed she didn't mention Rick Stetson. I left it alone. I figured she'd tell me if she wanted to. Then she floored me for a second time—

"Hey! How about we go up to Campbell Falls after dinner, just for old times?" I was astounded. We hadn't hung out in high school, but we both knew what Campbell Falls represented—a place to go to kiss and caress or maybe even have sex.

"Sure. Let me get the check." I tried not to rush, but I was pretty excited, let me tell you. On the drive up we didn't say much but she took my hand and rubbed it and commented on the new callouses I was developing—

"Bobby Westerland. Picking cabbages on my dad's farm. Ain't that somethin'."

"Just for the summer," I said.

"Where is that next school you're going to?"

"Illinois. It won't be as exciting as L.A., but it's where I got in, and Urbana-Champaign has a good engineering program."

"What are you going to be, a rocket scientist or something?"

"Maybe." In fact, I *was* studying propulsion systems, but I didn't tell her that. I didn't want to brag. I didn't want to do anything that would keep me from making out with Chloe Farnham at Campbell Falls, which was my high school fantasy come true. We got a little lost on the way out there, but finally arrived. The parking lot was empty. It was after 10:00 p.m. I pulled into a dark corner even the almost full moon didn't light up. Funny thing was, we didn't start kissing right away. We reminisced for a while, and talked more about our individual dreams. Chloe talked up her idea of bringing truckloads of organic vegetables to New York I let on that I hope to work for NASA someday. Why hadn't I ever been able to talk to Chloe (or any girl) like this when I was in high school? How different my life might have been! I knew about Campbell Falls, but I'd only been there once with a girl, Velma Snyder, and we'd hardly exchanged more than a few feeble kisses before she asked me to take her home. That evening had had a crushing impact on my fragile ego. I thought I must have been a pretty lousy date, and a bad kisser. But here I was five years later with Chloe Farnham, one of the so-called popular girls, and here we were nuzzling and sharing our most intimate thoughts with each other. Finally, we ran out of things to say to each other and began to kiss. It was great! I'd had a few girlfriends in California. I knew how to please a woman, and I thought I was doing a pretty good job at it. We weren't taking our clothes off yet but everything was getting a little disheveled when another car pulled into the parking lot, and suddenly a bright light shone in our windows. We pulled apart and tried to straighten up our clothing as blue flashing lights came on in addition to the floodlight. A large figure moved in front of the lights and approached my dad's pickup. The policeman was holding an oversized flashlight in his hand. I was blinded and put up a hand to shield my eyes from the glare.

"Aren't you two a little old for this sort of—" and then he stopped, because he suddenly realized who he was talking to—

"—Chloe? Chloe, what the hell are you doing out here? And who's—?"

"Hi Rick." I had recognized him immediately once he pointed the flashlight down. Except for the buzz-cut and maybe a little added weight, he looked exactly the same. So did I, I suppose. Better glasses, less obviously nerdy clothing, but not all that different from a few years ago in high school. I started to laugh because the whole thing was so funny. Rick didn't like that.

"Zip it, buster. You know it's illegal to park here after sunset."

"Oh come on, Rick. How many times were you and Chloe here our senior year, after you got your license?"

"Yeah come on, Rick," said Chloe. There was a distinct trace of bitterness in her voice. "Don't you still come out here with what's-her-name?"

"I'm not seeing her anymore—"

"So I heard—" said Chloe—

"—And even if I was I wouldn't come here. Jesus, grow up, the two of you."

There was no denying that in his policeman's uniform and with his military haircut Rick looked much more mature than either of us, and he had caught us. The whole thing was starting to be a bit weird for me.

"C'mon, Chloe, let's go." I reached for the ignition, but Rick wasn't finished with us yet.

"You go when I say you can go."

"What are you going to do? Arrest us for parking after dark? And how is that going to look in the Pittsfield newspaper? *'Policeman Arrests Ex-Girlfriend at Campbell Falls'.*" Chloe was taunting him. I realized the whole thing was a setup. Chloe had hoped Rick would catch us. She wanted him to see that she could get along fine without him. Without another word, Rick turned and walked to his patrol car. He followed us out of the parking lot and for a few miles, but eventually turned off. I dropped Chloe off at her dad's farm, worked for Bill Farnham for the rest of the summer and never saw her again. She wasn't interested in me. But I didn't care. I'd enjoyed the whole experience. The look on Rick Stetson's face when he recognized first Chloe and then me was worth it.

I graduated from Urbana at the very top of my class, and I did become an actual rocket scientist. I work for one of the Silicon Valley firms that's under contract with NASA to produce commercial space vehicles. Chloe got out of Southfield. She moved to New York, started her organics business, was quickly bought out by Whole Foods, and now runs their regional organics distribution chain. Rick's still a policeman in Southfield.

East Brookfield: A Field of Memory

vii

I would never have seen it if I hadn't wandered away from the music, stoned, a little dizzy (all that craft beer), and maybe the tiniest bit disgusted at the behavior of my fellow festival attendees. This year's East Brookfield Music Fest was turning into Woodstock without the rock stars and the love. We had the rain and the mud, and that was pretty much it.

I never would have seen it if I hadn't walked away from the fistfight after the first guy went down from a sucker punch to the jaw. They say that the fights you see on TV aren't real, that if you or I got hit with the kind of punches heroes do, we'd be out, not fighting anymore. That's what happened in this fight. Two big men, drunk,

and one of them more of a fighter than the other, decks
the other guy with one punch, and the other guy is out,
his friends trying to revive him while the first guy walks
away laughing.

I never would have seen it. I wish I'd never seen it. I'll
never forget it. There was a little pond on the property
next to the muddy field where the festival was taking
place. It was fenced off so the festival-goers wouldn't
swim in it, but somebody had jimmied the gate and a
small dock was accessible. No one else was down in this
corner of the festival. I walked out onto the planking, first
careful to pull the gate shut behind me. I wanted a little
time to myself, to sober up, get less high, put the ugly
fight scene out of my mind. I sat down cross-legged at the
end of the rickety wooden thing. A puff of wind rippled
the water, then it returned to a muddy stillness reflecting
the grey sky above. I felt a calm come over me. The
queasiness of the beer and the fight was subsiding,
replaced by a feeling of serenity.

Suddenly two divers rose out of the murky pond, right
off the dock where I sat. They were holding something
between them. A girl. Young, black, lifeless. They laid her
gently on the deck, clambered out, quickly shucked their
scuba gear, picked her up between them and ran off,
scarcely glancing at me. I sat there, stunned. What had
just happened? The pond had resumed is tranquil
aspect. My mind was reeling in chaos.

Later that night, back in my apartment, I wrote this poem about it:

death of a naiad
the concert was tedious,
bad covers of bad seventies songs.
i wandered down the hill
to the edge of an algae-fouled lake
and tip-toed out a rotting boat dock, alone.

i must have been there for five minutes
before the first diver rose
off to my right, no more than fifteen feet from the pilings,
and then the second, holding her in his arms,
that pale water nymph, hair streaming,
sightless eyes rolled back in her head.

they waved at me to help them
heave her surprisingly light body onto the platform
then rushed away without another word,
incongruous in their black rubber scuba suits,
scarcely taking time to kick off their flippers,
one cradling the girl,
one running on ahead
shouting for the ambulance.

as i came back up the hill, disoriented, crying,
a fistfight broke out
between two drunk, high concert-goers.
both were would-be martial artists,
big men, frighteningly powerful,

their fighting stylized--a punch, a block, a kick,
almost in slow motion. one was better than the other,
dazed his opponent with a strike,
knocked him down with a second.
he got up, staggering, face bloody.
then both ran away as the police rushed toward them
and I retched the remains of my picnic lunch.

the radio said she'd been resuscitated.
i didn't believe it.
later i heard she'd died.

oh naiad! you are supposed to be an immortal,
not an unattended child, lost on a summer afternoon.

Which memory is the truer one, the one I am telling
you now or the one in the poem I wrote immediately after
it happened? Does it matter? I'm troubled. I want to
know how I felt and I want to remember it truly and well.
I was just an observer with an altered sense of reality. A
little girl died. A man got his face smashed in. I did
nothing. The divers didn't ask me, and I didn't offer.

But the poem leaves out the most important detail.
Yes, I saw two divers emerge from the scummy waters of
the pond with the unconscious Naiad held between them.
But after the festival ended, after the ambulances took
away the girl and the injured fighter, after I had sobered
up enough, I drove myself back to my apartment.
Stupefied by the events of the day, I sat and watched
television mindlessly. Toward the end of a newscast a clip
from the festival played, and there was the girl being

carried off. She was dead now, they had been unable to revive her. And, oh my god, there I was, a dazed onlooker, looking stupid and ridiculous. I had been oblivious to the fact that there was a camera crew there. I ran to the bathroom and retched out the contents of the festival—beer, brats, fries, I puked it all up then, not after the fight like it says in the poem. But nothing could remove the bitter taste in my brain, the foul redolence of Death.

Sheffield: Shooting a Moose

viii

I'd been the animal control officer for Sheffield, Egremont, Great Barrington and New Marlborough for seven years when the incident I'm about to describe took place. It's not a glamour job, let me tell you. A lot of roadkill, a lot of angry trapped raccoons in crawlspaces. But it keeps me out and about and in nature, which I enjoy, and out of offices and cubicles, which I hate. I had a van issued by the county, and very little supervision. I'm a small woman in my fifties with greying hair, but I've kept fit by climbing all over the hills and valleys of Western Massachusetts. People call me and I take care of their animal problems, whatever they might be. I've rescued sick owls poisoned by eating mice that had consumed vegetables contaminated by pesticide. I've saved a few deer struck by cars, and other animals hurt through contact with human beings. Like an undertaker or an emergency room doctor, I've chosen to deal with the somewhat morbid nature of my work by affecting a cool response to everything. If I didn't do that, I'd go crazy from all the pain and suffering I see. Don't ever let anyone tell you animals don't feel pain. They do. Even fish. Trust me. Like the Buddhists say: *Even an ant treasures its life.* But the worst of it is contained in the story I'm going to tell you now, about the time I had to kill a moose.

Those of you with literary interests will immediately see echoes between my tale and *Shooting An Elephant* by George Orwell. Ironically, it's one of my favorite stories. Like Orwell, I was summoned to deal with a large, supposedly out of control beast. A moose had been spotted in fields near the village of Sheffield. It wasn't hard to find it. There was a crowd gathered and a docile animal who by all rights should have been just let alone. When I arrived in the vicinity, more than twenty cars were parked along the edge of the field, and a group of people were watching the moose, who was a good two hundred yards off. Moose sightings used to be common, but are becoming rarer. I parked my van and got out. I had a rifle I had no intention of using, just for self-protection. When I approached the moose, a large bull with an impressive rack, I saw the problem immediately. The moose had been shot. He had a gaping wound in his shoulder, and was mad with pain. There is no hunting season for moose in Massachusetts. It was early December, shotgun hunting season for deer, and some fool had mistaken the moose for a buck.

In *Shooting An Elephant*, Orwell realizes he must kill the elephant to save face as a member of the ruling colonial class. The hostile, excited Burmese crowd demands it, and they want the meat. In my case, the crowd of locals definitely did not want the moose to be shot. I didn't want to kill the moose either, for several reasons: I'm a woman who abhors senseless killing. I'm an animal control officer. My job is to help creatures, not kill them. I love moose. I wanted to make the assembled crowd happy and keep it alive. But I had to kill him. I edged up as close to the animal as I dared, and fired one shot from my Springfield .30-06. The great animal did not fall down immediately, but I knew I didn't need to fire another shot, thank god. I had finished him, unlike Orwell's elephant, which Orwell had to pour round after round into and never did stay around long enough to see it die. The moose crumpled slowly and ended up in an awkward crouch, legs folded under him where he remained for a minute or so. His last lung-punctured gasps were painfully audible. Finally, he fell over. I heard a commotion behind me. Several people were running toward me. Actually, almost the whole crowd of bystanders that had parked their cars to view this magnificent creature, and hadn't expected to witness a killing, were now hurrying through the field to where I stood next to the body of the moose.

"Why did you do that? Why did you kill him?!" they were shouting. I carefully put the safety on my rifle and lowered it, wishing I had the case with me and not in the van. I waited until everyone arrived at the spot where the beast lay dead.

"Did you have to do that?"

"Couldn't you have used a tranquilizer?" They demanded to know why I'd done what I'd done. They encircled me and the dead moose. That was okay. I'd given lots of lectures as a park ranger, another outdoor job I'd held until budget cuts hosed it.

"All right, listen up everyone." I straightened up my uniform up a little, and would have liked to have brushed my hair but that was not possible. "A crime has been committed here."

"Yeah, you shot a moose!"

"The moose had already been shot. There's no hunting season for moose. We consider it a crime, cruelty to animals."

"But why did you have to shoot him, Sheila?"

"It was my neighbor Hugh. We knew each other by first name. He understood what was going on, and he lobbed me a softball question to help me.

"He was dying, and he was in great pain. Look, Game Laws require hunters to make every effort to find the animal. Obviously, this person realized they'd shot a protected species, and chose to run away instead of doing the right thing."

That quieted the crowd down. Now they turned their attention more fully to the fallen moose.

"Thanks for putting it out of its misery," someone said quietly. I nodded. But it didn't make me feel that much better. Gradually, after they took a few respectful cell phone photos (none with me in them, I assure you) the crowd dissipated. Everybody went back to their cars and drove off, leaving me with a thousand-pound dead moose to deal with. I called for a bigger truck. And a winch. Later I looked for footprints or tire tracks, but the moose could've been shot anywhere, it might have run five miles and only given out here in this field in Sheffield. It was a crime. The criminal was going to get away with it, and there was nothing I could do about it. We did not stuff the moose head as a trophy for somebody's wall. Instead, with the field owner's permission, we dug a deep pit with a backhoe and buried the moose right there. I go out there sometimes. You can't see a thing. The machine dug deep and then filled up the hole it had made, and the grass and weeds at the edge of the field grew back quickly. In one season all sign of what had happened there was gone. I made my own little marker there, a couple of stones that were out of the farmer's way and too heavy for an ordinary person to have any reason to move. To me they symbolize everything that was lost that day when a moose was shot twice for no good reason.

South Deerfield: Murder at the Dancehall

For eight thousand years Native American tribes have lived on and around the small hill they call Wequamps, in myth, as seen from the river, the body of a giant beaver who ate humans. The colonial settlers called it Sugarloaf because that's what it looked like to them. In the late nineteenth century, the Poles came to grow and pick onions. The landscape reminded them of their homeland. The town gained a kielbasa-tinged flavor and lost some of its English reserve. There was polka at the dance pavilion at the foot of the little mountain. A carriage road led to the Summit House hotel on top. If you walk up Sugarloaf today there is no trace of the hotel. When the pavilion was torn down, some of its floorboards were repurposed as the flooring of the new Thayer Market that is now the BBA Deli, with twenty kinds of kielbasa. That's the local legend, but it's not the whole story. Buried beneath the pavilion were traces of an unsolved mystery that has only deepened with time. No one remembered, no one cared, it was three generations in the past, but Mrs. Edna Melnicky had a story to tell. When she heard from her niece Linda, a friend of mine, that I was researching the old dance place, she told Linda to arrange for me to interview her.

"Mrs. Melnicky remembers taking the trolley out to the pavilion at the base of Mount Sugarloaf and dancing there," Linda told me. "I'm sure she could be a big help to you. For a story, I mean." Linda was a real estate agent. I agreed to interview Mrs. Melnicky, even though I had no particular use for the story. I'm not a newspaper columnist or a crime reporter. I write little internet posts that sometimes get published here and there. Maybe Edna would be enough of a character to rate a human-interest piece

Edna Melnicky wanted to make sure that the tale she had to tell did not end with her passing, and Linda had convinced me that I go see Mrs. Melnicky and hear her out. We agreed to meet at the Senior Center on Main Street in South Deerfield. Linda gave me a little background on her before we went. Edna Tomazak had married George Melnicky in the late Forties. They had sixty years of marriage together. She worked at Yankee Candle for many years. George had died a few years ago, and Edna still lived by herself in a tiny apartment behind the South Deerfield Police Department. She walked to the

Senior Center a few times a week, and liked to attend lectures and educational events more than bingo.

Linda said she would come with me but bowed out at the last minute, I think deliberately. I think Mrs. Melnicky wanted it that way.

When I arrived at the Senior Center Mrs. Melnicky was seated at a small table by herself in the main meeting room. Edna Melnicky's first words to me were:

"I killed him."

"I beg your pardon?"

"I killed him. I never told anyone, but it's time now. I'll be gone soon. Everyone else who knew the story is dead, and someone should know."

I stood there for a minute, confused and amazed, studying Mrs. Melnicky's pleasant, unremarkable old Polish lady's face.

"May I sit down?"

"Promise you will take this old woman seriously when she tells you the story."

"I promise."

I slid into a chair opposite Edna Melnicky. It seemed unlikely that there could be an unsolved murder in South Deerfield that wasn't some known part of the town lore. I had never heard of one. But here before me was this tiny woman with blue hair in curls, glasses, pug nose, a handsome and dignified elder who must have been beautiful in her younger days.

I put a writing pad on the table and started to take out the miniature tape recorder I use for interviews.

"No tape recorder. You have to use your memory."

She took my hands in hers, and gazed at me with watery but still sharp blue eyes. And then she told me this story:

"We used to go dancing at the Pavilion. The trolley from town ran right out there. All the farm boys would come in for it on a Saturday night. Some of them were 'fresh off the boat', we used to say, guys who could barely speak English, mostly Polish. Big strong men. Bad dancers. But we had fun. The pavilion was just a low-roofed building with sides that could open up on hot nights. The Polish men would come in smelling of dirt and onions, and we'd hold our noses, but after a couple drinks and a few dances, nobody cared what anybody smelled like."

Mrs. Melnicky fell silent for a moment, gazing vacantly out onto the street where she saw backward sixty years and more.

"Please go on," I said gently. She was still holding my hands.

"This was during the war years, you know. Death was all around us. Most of the South Deerfield boys were away in the war. Young Polish immigrants made up the difference in the labor force. One night there was this young man I liked. This was before I met George. This young man was very forward, he was in a hurry, but I liked his black hair and his black eyes and I thought I could trust him. He took a fancy to me. He was an undocumented alien, no papers, and gave me only his first name: Janusz. He couldn't speak much English, only Polish. He'd come to the pavilion two or three Saturdays in a row and I'd danced with him a couple of times, when one evening he asked me in broken English if I would like to take a stroll. So, I did. We did. Up the carriage road, and off into the woods a little bit. It was pretty steep. We couldn't go far off it. He wanted to kiss me. I was all right with that, but then he wanted more, and I told him to stop, but he didn't. He pushed me down, and started to lift up my dress, you know. I was scratching him and squirming around, and my hand landed on a rock, and I picked it up and smashed him. I must have hit him just right, a pressure point or a vulnerable soft spot, or maybe he had a condition. I killed him right then and there. He went limp. I pushed him off me." Mrs. Melnicky stopped. She was again staring backward in time. I gave her a moment to compose herself. She let go of my hands and continued.

"I tried to straighten myself up as best as I could and then staggered back down the hill to the dance. As soon as I walked in, my friend Jeanie came over to me and asked me what happened. I must have looked a sight. She took me into the Ladies to clean up, and then she got my two other close friends, Monika and Buddy, and together they brought me outside and to a corner of the property out of the light. I told them what happened, between sobs. It was awful. I thought my life was over. Monika and Jeanie comforted me, but Buddy took command. Later that summer he'd drop out of school when he turned 18 and go into the Army Air Force, and get shot down and lost forever somewhere in the South Pacific. But that night he was my hero. *'Tell no one else, understand? No one. Not tonight, not ever'*, he said, and we all nodded. The four of us slipped away from the pavilion and scrambled up to the body. Only those three people knew about it: Buddy, and Jeanie, and Monika. And none of them ever said anything about it again, to me or anyone else. We kept the secret to our graves, or at least they did. And now I'm telling you."

"You don't think Janusz is traceable back to a missing person report or anything?"

"Nobody in our town knew his name. He was just Janusz. The farm owner where he worked probably thought he'd run off back to the big city. Nobody came looking for him or inquiring after him. There was never any investigation. He just vanished."

"You and your friends buried him on the hillside?" I asked.

"No," she said. "Buddy said we couldn't dig a grave fast enough and deep enough that the animals wouldn't mess it up and expose it."

"What did you do?"

"We put him in the dance pavilion. Or under it. Buddy was one of the weekend employees, a summer job. After everybody left that night, we went back up and Buddy wrapped up Janusz in some leftover canvas and we half-carried half-dragged him down to the pavilion (it took the four of us) and into the crawlspace beneath the dance floor, and buried him there. People complained about a slight "dead animal" smell for a while, but it passed eventually. And that would have been the end of it except—"

"Except—?"

"Except he, Janusz, is still right over there somewhere at the foot of Sugarloaf."

"When they tore down the dance hall in 1946, after the war, wouldn't they have found him then?"

"That's what I thought. Oh, I was so terrified for weeks during that demolition. But nothing happened. Maybe he'd decomposed enough and the squirrels and whatnot had gotten to the body and there wasn't much left. Maybe Buddy had moved him. Maybe Janusz got crushed in the rubble of the tear-down. I don't know, and I don't want to know. I just wanted someone else to know about this before I died."

"You shouldn't feel guilty, Mrs. Melnicky. You were defending yourself against rape. Today you'd be a hero to many women."

"Oh, I didn't feel particularly guilty, for the reason you mentioned. But I felt sad. This young man had such an unknown, ignominious resting place."

"You never told Mr. Melnicky?"

"I never told George. I didn't want to burden him."

I looked at Mrs. Melnicky tenderly. "I don't know whether to say '*your secret is safe with me*' or something else. What do you want me to do with this story?"

"Remember."

"Of course I'll remember. But what else?"

"When I'm gone, which won't be long now, then you can do whatever you feel is right."

Mrs. Melnicky lived another eleven months. We never spoke again. So here it is, Edna Melnicky's confession to a murder. I looked half-heartedly in local newspapers and even in the Boston and New York papers from the time for any stories of missing Janusz's, but as Mrs. Melnicky suspected, there was nothing. I fully believed her story.

She had no reason to lie to me or make up this tale. She told it lucidly and cogently. For sixty years there were only four who knew, and at the end only Mrs. Melnicky, and then me, and now all of you know.

Northfield: A Northfield Girl and a Drum Circle

When I was fifteen years old, I was a sophomore at Northfield School for Girls in Northfield, Massachusetts. Chapel twice a day, grave of the founder Dwight Lyman Moody perched on the highest piece of land on the property, with a view up the Connecticut River valley to Vermont. I was a lonely girl, given to staying in my room as much as possible. I didn't have a boyfriend at the boys' school Mount Hermon. Maybe it was because I was late to puberty and still flat-chested, with a sharp nose and a narrow, horsey face, or maybe it was my shyness and my introspective nature, but no one came to make idle chat and try to feel my knee when the housemother wasn't looking, in the parlor of my dorm in Marquand

Hall. Parlor dates. Ugh! I had taken to making long walks off campus. I would wander down the hill into town and beyond. Sometimes I crossed farm fields to gain access to the river. Other times I followed old trails into the woods off Route 63. I never thought about danger—I was too preoccupied with my own internal conflicts. Back then a girl could walk in far fields without fear of molestation, most of the time anyway. And of course, I was two hundred and fifty years removed from the time when Native Americans (we called them Indians then) from the Squakeag, Nashaway, or Quaboag tribes might threaten a white settler.

In town I often stopped at the Super IGA to buy milk that I left on the windowsill of my room as a makeshift refrigerator, so that I could have my cold cereal when I wanted it in the morning, and not that sickly grey glue they called oatmeal in the dining hall. One morning in the store I heard two men talking about fishing:

"Went up to Maine with the sister-in-law out on Moosehead."

"Catch anything interesting?"

"Trout. Double–digits every day. No salmon, though."

"But them trout, on the grill, nothin' bettah."

"You know it."

I wanted to go with them. I wished I was the sister-in-law. It was unusual the two fishermen mentioned a woman at all. She must be something special. But why 'the sister-in-law' and not 'the wife'? I stumbled out of the Super IGA with my wax carton of milk, thinking about trout fishing from a canoe on a lake in Maine—the stillness, the cold, the soft glimmery water stretching grey and misty to stands of pines on small islands miles away, floating like faery castles above the fog-shrouded, mirror-smooth lake. I was not a bad fisherman myself, with an ordinary rod and a bobber on a pond, or a thick string wrapped around my finger and a lead sinker off the rocks at the ocean. But those fishermen weren't interested in me, except maybe as a curio. Their lives and the lives of the girls at Northfield rarely intersected. A few of them might be maintenance workers on campus, or delivery men. That was about it. Those four years at Northfield were the loneliest of my life, yet I wouldn't trade them for anything. I got an excellent education that has served me well for forty years and more, and I learned about myself. Men, marriage and all that came much later. Back then I was on my own, one among several hundred girls. I steered my own course, made my own path, in ways I could never do now. Maybe it was the times, the general loosening that was taking place in America, but when my parents dropped me off in September of my first year I felt like I was cutting all ties with the known. I felt free, even with the strictures and almost regimental routine of the school, with its bells and its rules and its traditions and its religion.

On one of my solitary rambles I came across the granite marker commemorating one of the battles between the natives and the colonials. It stood on the roadside of Route 63 where I was walking, and read about Indian council fires and a massacre. Not far from that sign was another marker that read:

On this plain, Captain Richard Beers and his men were surprised by Indians Sept. 4, 1675. Some little ways on, his grave had another marker that said in part: *His monument is on the mountain-side above.* A few old cars were parked along the side of the road, but I didn't see anyone around. I decided to walk in and take a look at the council fires. I followed a path from the wood's edge into the forest. It was late spring, and the woods were growing lushly green, like a rain forest, with ferns on the ground and oaks fully clothed. The trail led straight into the woods. It was more like an old logging road than a footpath, wide enough for vehicles, with old tire ruts, but no one had driven a car or truck in here for many years. Young firs were starting to grow up in the underbrush. It looked like nobody came back here. In twenty years there wouldn't be a trail.

I was walking along when all of a sudden, a man appeared right in front of me. He was dressed in buckskin head to toe—shirt, leggings, and moccasins. And his face was covered in paint, a garish, ferocious mask.

I shrieked, and the man had to restrain himself from leaping forward to put a hand over my mouth. He put a finger to his lips in the universal gesture for silence, and spoke not a word to me. But I ignored his plea for quietness and asked him right out:

"What are you, like from the Renaissance Fair or something?"

He carried an old-fashioned muzzle-loader, but I happened to know it wasn't primitive weapons hunting season.

The man twitched his finger at me, not annoyed but slightly impatient, and gestured for me to follow him silently forward. I fell in behind, not knowing what else to do. I wasn't afraid of him, I just wanted to know why the costume. We walked single file like that for another couple hundred yards, and then I heard the low muffled pounding of drum, and voices chanting. *Okay this is getting weird*, I thought. But I didn't turn around. We moved forward more slowly and cautiously. *This is a fun game.*

The man in buckskin turned back to me. He had a soft brown beard but hard brown eyes. He crouched lower, and I saw him draw a large knife with his right hand from a sheath on his left side. He waved me up, and I knelt beside him. He pulled back a few fern fronds and showed me the source of the sound. In a clearing not thirty yards from where we hid, a group of men were sitting or standing in a ragged circle around a pretty massive bonfire. It was a warm afternoon; the fire was unnecessary for heating or cooking at the moment. It was just there as the centerpiece for the dancing and music. The members of the group were not all in costume; some were dressed like local farmers in jeans and flannel shirts and John Deere caps. At least I knew I hadn't fallen into some time travel black hole. Others wore headdresses but no other parts of an outfit, and a few were fully decked out in Native American regalia. Some of them looked like Indians, or at least my conception of Indians, having had no experience with them previously. Some looked like the guys who hang around check cashing places on Friday.

I saw the buckskin man making hand signals, and I realized that he and I were not alone. At least a half-dozen other men, also in varying degrees of colonial-era historical get-up formed an outer ring around the fire circle and the men surrounding it. Were the faux colonials actually going to attack the faux council fire Indians? I couldn't believe it. But that's what happened. At a signal from him, the whites burst into the clearing, whooping and leaping. The Indians, at first stunned, quickly took up the challenge with loud war cries of their own, and a standoff ensued. The white men were outnumbered probably three to one, but they were young and athletic while the council fire men were mostly older and sedentary. I heard a lot of cursing, which didn't bother me as much as it would have my dorm mistress. But to my great relief it looked like nothing more would happen than some shouting. Both sides soon tired of it, and stood facing each other.

"What the f#@k, Junior? What's this all about?" said one of the older Indians, a portly gentleman whose only concession to costume was a beaded headband and a grey ponytail.

"My name's not Junior. It's Ebenezer Freeman," my buckskin guide said.

"No, it ain't," the Indian said. "It's Timmy Woodside. I pick apples in your father's orchard some seasons. And you know me."

"Sure, I do. You're old Harold Rance."

"That's right. So, what's all this with the war paint and the weapons, Timmy?"

"Ah, Christ, Harold. We're just playin' around on a weekend."

"Playing around? This is a sacred space. Get the f#@k off it."

"Sacred what? Looks like a bunch of lost old men. Anyway, this is state land. You don't own it."

"The state don't own it either."

A very old man, not dressed in costume, stood up, removed his baseball cap, and began to speak. The other Indians stopped their cries and listened to him respectfully. "My ancestor Massasoit, a Wampanoag sachem, said: *What is this you call property? It cannot be the earth, for the land is our mother, nourishing all her children, beasts, birds, fish and all men. The woods, the streams, everything on it belongs to everybody and is for the use of all. How can one man say it belongs only to him?*"

"Ah, f#@k that. Look what happened to Massasoit. He helped the Pilgrims, and His son King Philip—"

—"Metacomet—"

"—Whatever—lost a war and fifty years later there were hardly any Wampanoags left."

"We're still here. Four hundred years of oppression and we're still here. There's a Wampanoag reservation on Martha's Vineyard."

"Yeah, so's you can build a casino out there."

"That'd be one way to win back some of the white man's money!"

Off to the side there was a scuffle. One of the Indians had tried to take a knife away from one of the young men who'd been weaving it in his face. I didn't see what happened (for which I was thankful later, at the trial) but I heard a real cry of pain and surprise that was different from the war whoops that had filled the forest air a few minutes before; and then one of the Indians fell to the ground face forward. His companions rushed to him and turned him over. His face was bloody from falling on his nose, but it was the bloom of red spreading on his shirt that scared me. His breath was coming in gasps and rattles, and then not at all. We all stood there stunned, me, the Native Americans, the town boys whose prank had just ruined their lives.

"Stupid f#@kin' Czestowicz! What the hell were you thinking?" Timmy Woodside, my forest companion yelled in the face of the boy still holding the dripping knife.

"He tried to take my blade, man. F$#k. I didn't mean to—"

"—He's dead. Somebody call 911."

Czestowicz threw the knife into the woods (the police found it within minutes) and the whites withdrew a few paces but none of them tried to run away. Maybe they were too astonished and stupefied to act, or maybe they knew it wouldn't make a difference. Timmy Woodside sat down next to me with his head in his hands.

"All we meant to do was frighten them. Look, I don't even have any ammunition for this old thing. It just shoots fire when I set it off. Jesus!" Timmy was crying. I put an arm around his shoulder gently. The Native America group had stripped the shirt off the dead man and were examining his wound, while one of them cradled his head and called out his name over and over—

"—Bobby. Bobby. Bobby." I learned later his full name was Bobby "Nosy Porcupine" Devens, a local man who ran a powwow every year up off Route 2 in Charlemont.

From far off we could hear police sirens. Nobody ran, they all just waited together for the cops to come stumbling and rampaging through the woods, totally unlike the creeping ambush I had witnessed. Three of them, guns drawn, burst into the clearing and ordered everybody's hands up. One of them, obviously trained as an EMT, went immediately to Devens, who lay sprawled on the ground surrounded by his fellow council fire dancers and singers. He was dead, there could be no doubt, but that didn't stop Patrolman Hodgkins from trying CPR on him while a second patrolman radio'ed for an ambulance. They were going to take us all in, Native Americans and whites and me too, but Timmy told the patrolman—

"—This girl ain't part of it. She was just walking in the woods at the wrong time—" so they let me go, but we all walked out of the woods together in two discrete groups and one of the patrolmen gave me a ride back to campus and a warning not to wander around in the woods alone, which I continued to do through the rest of my time at Northfield School for Girls.

The local boys received 10-year sentences for second degree manslaughter because it was determined that Bobby Devens died of a heart attack, not a knife wound. They were out in six years with time off for good behavior. By that time I had graduated college and was living in a crappy apartment off Commonwealth in Boston and grinding my way through an entry level job at a public housing non-profit of which I am now the CEO.

Once a year for the past forty-some years I have gone out to Charlemont to sit in a circle with the sons and daughters of the men I had met only once in the woods on a very sad day. They tell the story of the day Nosy Porcupine got stabbed, and many other stories. I am welcomed, perhaps because they know my story, perhaps because they sense what my walking has brought me in the way of simple wisdom. They sing, they dance, and I sit and sway and feel my connection to a ring of charred stones a few miles to the south and east and across the big Quinetucket River.

Plainfield: An Episode at Earthdance

I never saw the center of Plainfield. My ride took me
straight to Earthdance, where a group of young,
energetic, incredibly fit, and, as I found out, slightly crazy
body-centered movement artists lived, worked, and
danced. I was coming for a three-weeks intensive
residency as a "Visiting Teacher." Theoretically I didn't
have to do as much work as the people who lived there,
but my plan was to participate as fully as possible in
their day-to-day experience, and bring that into the work.
I'd had a solo show in a theater in New York the previous
summer—Fiona Elspeth in *Screaming Scottish Fire*, in
which I danced a number of pieces based on a red-haired
woman warrior of the past, Queen Scathach of Skye,

whose battle yells were legendary. I was something of a hot property in the dance world. When I arrived at Earthdance in the dead of winter, no red carpet was rolled out for me. I was given a bunk in a shared room in the dorm space, and left by myself in the rustic accommodation. A pile of funky sheets and blankets lay by the door. I made up my own bed, and went to the dorm-style shared bathroom and wet some paper towels so I could clean off the dusty side table next to my bed. A small lamp with a torn lampshade sat on the table. It didn't work when I tried it. As the early darkness fell, I had to make do with the single bare bulb dangling from an old-fashioned cord overhead. It was a couple hundred yards walk in the snow from the dorm to the main house where the two dance spaces were located. It was also where everyone cooked, ate and hung out. I waited until it was almost dinnertime to go down to the main house. No one made any formal introduction or welcomed me. Being a forward Scot, I made the first move.

"Hi! I'm Fiona," I said to a tattoo'ed, bearded young man who was peeling potatoes in the cramped kitchen.

"Hey. I'm Rick."

"Can I help?"

"Sure." He put me to work filling pots for boiling the potatoes and rinsing them as he peeled them. Other dancers wandered in. There didn't seem to be any timetable for the meal. Someone put out silverware and dishes. Two other people brought out a huge casserole and another two made salad. Music was playing, rhythmic and lively, the kind of music you can't help but dance to, and everybody was lithe and limber and moving their young bodies to the beat. I was maybe ten years older than most of them, a real tribal elder. I knew they knew who I was. My wild unbraided Scot red hair gave me away to anyone with any familiarity with the dance world. Gradually each of them introduced themselves to me, but not in any orderly or formal fashion, just as part of preparing the meal. The dining room table was a couple of outdoor picnic tables that had been brought indoors. I marveled at the dedication of these young dancers, who were here to study and grow, and party!

After dinner I was exhausted from my trip and wanted to go lie down, but instead I was almost literally dragged by the group, through a smaller space called the Dance Barn, rectangular and lined with windows to let in the light, and into the nearly circular main dance space called the Umbrella Studio because of its unique tent-like canvas interior ceiling. Everyone lay down, and I thought briefly this might be my opportunity for some rest, but it turned out they were just limbering up, going through a series of stretches led by Jenna, a young blonde beauty with an amazingly flexible body. Some of the warm-ups I recognized from dance, others from yoga, and others were weird for me, like lying on my back and shaking my hands and legs, which Jenna called the "Dying Cock-roach." And then music was put on, an evening raga over hidden loudspeakers, and everyone started moving, always maintaining touch with at least one other person in a sensual but not overtly sexy way. Instead of trying to teach or lecture, I just let myself be drawn in by this little band, all of whom knew each other's bodies and souls intimately, that much was clear. It was almost as if I was auditioning for the job they'd already hired me for. That was okay. I could play with the best of them! Despite years of practice and performance, I'd never danced in a circular space like the Umbrella. As in Dance Barn studio, it was lined with windows, and even though it was dark out now, the combination of its shape and the openness of the many windows gave the space a unique almost planetarium-like quality of spaciousness and openness. The contact improv dancing morphed into a whirling dervish kind of movement, everyone spinning and twirling, and that led to a seemingly endless series of kicks and jumps, the music growing ever more frenetic, twenty of us leaping around in anarchic yet beautiful rhythm. The young people went on dancing, on and on and on, into the wee hours. Finally, I stopped and just watched for a while, picking out dancers whose particular traits I could use in the next three weeks of my residency. At last I quietly left the room and walked in the blackness of a new moon over crunching snow to my dorm room. As I lay in my plain bed I could still hear the music. They danced until almost dawn. I never thought anyone could have more energy than me. They all did.

The next morning, we had our first official residency session. I'd called my workshop *Dance Back to Nature*. Maybe that's why they'd picked me from hundreds of teachers offering workshops. We were going to explore through dance how climate change and human beings' continuing alteration of nature might be influenced by dance. It was ambitious. Why would anyone think that simply dancing could be an activist statement, or cause any real change in the world? When we gathered in the late morning I asked each person in the room to give their answer to that question, and I told them I would ask them again at the end of three weeks. They weren't a particularly articulate group—they expressed themselves much better through their bodies than their words, but they were honest and passionate, and that's all that mattered. We stood in a circle in the circular Umbrella Studio and went around the room, starting with Karen to my left:

Karen (nose ring, chi pants, black hair, T-Shirt that read: "Dance First Think Later"): "*I just know the Earth is in trouble, and I want to help.*"

Kwame (black, shaved head, muscular body, wicked pissah Boston accent): "*We gotta dance back into it. Used ta be dancers had powah. They wuh Shamans, they could make change through magic. That's what I want!*"

Rick (the cook from last night, dazzling blue eyes, blonde ringlets and beard, a real satyr look): "*I wanna make love to the earth, the water, the sky, the colors. Dance lets me do that.*"

Johanna (Small but fiery. The most loquacious of the bunch) Likes to be tossed in the air by male dancers so she can fly!) "*I want you to show me how to make my dance meaningful, not just as art but as an instrument of war against the polluters, the destroyers, the desecrators.*"

Monika (the Polish Princess. Shy in speech (the accent) but expressive in movement. A little arrogant. Tall, thin, wispy blonde, angular face and features.) "*This is the most important work I will ever do. Please help me do that.*"

I loved them all already. I knew five things from teaching for several years: 1) Go slowly, 2) Never criticize anyone individually, 3) Leave all your personal troubles outside the studio, 4) Teach with Love, and 5) Don't share everything. Always leave them wanting a little more.

We started by taping sheets of paper to the walls and drawing out our ideas. They were a little better at drawing than speaking, but not much. I could tell they were a little frustrated that they weren't dancing yet. *'Though this be madness, yet there is method in it'*, I told them. I was making them hungry. They danced too much, in my opinion, and should save something for performance. I was drawing from them a more clear and visible expression of their ideas and desires. A mural emerged, a giant whale swimming in a sea of plastic garbage. It was powerfully sad, but when we came to dance it, became an oceanic allegory of hope. For the next three weeks we would develop and refine the idea into a powerful physical statement of the state of the world of Nature, and how we could heal Her, for Nature in its purest form is the expression of the Feminine, the physical form, as manifested in the Receptive, the dark, Yin, yet always in union with the Masculine, the spiritual form, the Creative, the light, Yang.

After one disastrous affair early in my teaching career, I had made it a personal rule never to date a student. This allowed me to remain completely objective when evaluating dancers in competitive situations. If the loose and playful group at Earthdance found me a little stiff and standoffish, that was okay. They began to appreciate my passion as much as what I was teaching them. They wanted to help me achieve the fullest demonstration of my assertions, and in that way, we helped each other. I was the teacher and as always happens when the teaching takes wing, I learned so much over these weeks.

"Tell us about your necklace, Fiona," Johanna asked as we all lay on the floor after one particularly grueling session where we made dolphin-like undulations for hours, trying to become like a pod, moving in unison. I glanced down at the necklace, a large deep blue lapis lazuli crystal with a mandala embedded in it, and the word "OM" written in Sanskrit in the center of the mandala:

I never took it off except to shower or bathe, which is probably why it had attracted the attention of the group, or at least of Johanna.

"It was a present from my teacher," I said. "He was an Indian man, Raj Manusha. Perhaps you've heard of him?" Of course they had. Raj had been a rising star in the dance world until he was shot and killed trying to stop a robbery at his father's grocery store in Queens. I had studied with Raj for several years. We'd been lovers briefly. "Raj gave it to me to remind me that the universe loves us all."

"Does it give you power?" Rick asked.

"It reminds me of Raj, so in that way, yes, it makes me feel like my teacher is still watching over me, even though he's gone."

"He's not gone," Kwame chimed in. "He just moved to another dimension."

We danced, and danced, and danced some more. I corrected a few minor imperfections in technique among the Earthdancers, but mostly I tried to keep them focused on dance as a way to save Mother Earth. I wanted them to learn to express themselves not just in unalloyed joy which they had in excess but in movements that conveyed the meanings and complexities we had developed. Our initial talks and drawings took form in dance. The dancers came together as a group in new ways. Outside there were days of pure whiteness, snow falling continuously for days, and nights of no snow and shimmering clarity, almost as light as day when the waxing moonlight filled the forest around us.

On the last night of the workshop we held a public performance in the Umbrella. The attendees were Earthdance donors, other dancers, and a few farmers and townspeople of Plainfield, looking uncomfortable and out of sorts among the extremely wealthy supporters and the extremely healthy dancers. It wasn't a huge crowd, but large enough that it gave the evening the feeling of a real performance. A student in the Film department at Hampshire was videotaping with decent equipment. My dancers gave amazing performances. Kwame and Monika in particular had internalized the piece. They were able to dance with fire, energy, and joy. One of them playfully copied and threw in my signature shriek from *Screaming*

Scottish Fire. They had practiced the basic moves until they could improvise freely. The audience gave us a standing ovation!

The threat of another storm sent people into the night almost immediately afterward. The Earthdancers were exhilarated and ready to party, but I was spent. I'd given them everything I had in the last three weeks. I was done. I longed for the comfort and privacy of my apartment in the city. When I saw them gearing up for another long jam dance session after the audience cleared out, I begged off and went back to my room. I stripped down, wrapped my abundant red hair in a towel, put another around my body, which was not young but still strong and toned. I couldn't remember being happier. I had imparted something, passed something along. Tribal elder, indeed! I walked to the common bathroom and took a shower. The heat and hot water, which had been iffy during my stay, cooperated for once, and I lingered under the soothing spray for a few minutes, reflecting on all we'd done. When I went back to my room, I sensed that something was wrong.

My purse was right there on the wobbly night-table, and no money had been taken. My credit cards were still there, and my god, my phone and expensive wristwatch were laying there. Something was missing. My necklace. The thief had known the sentimental value the mantra necklace held for me. It could only be one of the Earthdance dancers. I decided immediately not to bring it up to the group. I thought of my old teacher and lover Raj, felt his touch, saw his smile. Raj wouldn't have wanted me to spoil the beautiful group feeling that we had created in the last three weeks. Why let the actions of one person ruin that memory for everyone?

The next morning, we all hugged, said our goodbyes, and went our separate ways. I saw a few of them in New York in the following months, but nothing came of our workshop. It wasn't important enough to be mounted in a dance studio in New York. Six months after my residency at Earthdance, I received a package in the mail. It was so small I didn't even have to go to the Post Office to pick it up—it fit in the tiny mailbox of my tiny Brooklyn apartment. I opened the note first. It was written on faintly perfumed pink paper: *"I'm sorry I took this. I just had to have something from you since I couldn't have your heart. It has been a talisman to me, but I realized I should give it back to you. Even now, as I place it in this small box with this note, I can feel its power. Someday I hope to dance like you."*

The note was unsigned. I opened the small box and the deep blue of the necklace sparkled in my palm.

One of the Earthdance dancers had fallen in love with me, and hadn't said anything to me or tried to express their feelings to me in any physical way. I thought back to those weeks in the woods and the snow. Was it a man or a woman? Passionate Rick? Fragile Monika? One of the others? I didn't know. I knew that taking my necklace had not been an act of thievery but an affirmation of the strength and success of my teaching. I had fallen in love with all of them. To me they represented the hope of the world.

East Deerfield: A Night in the Caboose Bar

Wade had called it a bar, but by that time it was just a place for him and his friends to drink. He knew it wouldn't last more than a year or two; the money would run out. He figured then he'd run out too, or run down, or run away. Every night he opened at seven and they drank until two. If guys came in they didn't know, he'd serve them (it was always men) but there wasn't any conversation, nothing inviting, and pretty soon they left and never came back. It was just him and five or six friends, pretending to run a bar called *The Caboose*, in an abandoned last car on a siding underneath abandoned grain elevators down there in the rail yard on the upper end of River Road in East Deerfield. Once it had been a thriving place, boys sent out to bring buckets of beer to thirsty engineers and coal shovelers, meatloaf dinners for fifty-five cents, drafts for fifteen cents, a buck a bucket. Now it was nothing, and they were nothing, and their town was nothing, but at least they had this place, for now, where they could drink. So, there they were, every night, usually the same six of them: Wade, in his flannel shirt with the sleeves cut off to display his muscled arms and Semper Fi tattoo. Jake, the retired rail engineer, with the requisite small-bill blue striped cap and a big hard belly he stuffed into suspender-ed overalls. Al and Jim, two Gulf War vets, grungy, overweight, looking like nobody's taking care of them. Monty, a middle-aged loser who dressed like he was stuck in the seventies; and Ray, a younger guy. Lean, muscled. Wired tight. Clenched jaw.

One night, it could have been any night, Wade brought over two beers and set them in front of Al and Jim.

"Are you two faggots still living together?"

"Jesus, Wade, cut us a break. We're not gay. *'Not that there's anything wrong with that'*, like Seinfeld says."

Jim grunted a bitter laugh.

"We have to share a house because our wives left us."

"For each other? Lesbians, huh?"

"No, Wade. Jesus, don't start that kind of rumor. It'll be all over the Valley next."

"Don't worry. What happens in The Caboose stays in The Caboose."

Jake, who'd been listening from a couple stools down, chimed in—

"Hell, Wade. This ain't no Vegas. Where's the neon? Where's the free champagne? Where's the showgirls?"

"Champagne? That'd be like soda-pop to guys like you. —And I'm not even—"

—From down at the end of the bar the younger guy, Ray, called out—

"F@#k ya, man, pass the pickled eggs."

Jake turned away from Wade and to Ray.

"Ray, forchrissakes, do you have to start every sentence with 'F@#k ya'?"

Ray sneered. "F@#k ya, anybody got a cigarette?"

Ray wasn't a vet or a cop. Nobody knew what he did for money. He scared the older men, but they let him stay because he stood for drinks regularly. When he'd had one too many they steered clear of him. Wade always asked him to leave his weapons in the pickup he parked out back. Monty waved a bill from the other end of the bar.

"No more beer, Wade, man. Gimme a whisky."

"It wasn't the beer got you kicked off the force, Monty. Or the whisky either. It was selling meth and crushed opioids to the down and outs in town."

"If they didn't hang out here because it's the local county seat and the social services are all here, I wouldn't have no clientele and I wouldn't do it."

"What're you trying to do, get rid of them one overdose at a time?"

"Nah. Narcan stopped all that. Now they can OD over and over and the EMTs bring 'em back to life. It's like a zombie movie."

Monty made a face and walked around the bar like a zombie. Nobody laughed. From his stool Jake gave a signal that probably meant something when he was in the cab of a train. Wade turned to him—

"Whaddaya want, Jake? You ain't in the rail yard now, you know that."

"I just wanted to tell you how much I appreciate this crumb box. This buggy is like a second home to me." It was hard to tell if he was being a sentimental drunk or sarcastic.

"Yeah, a rest home. Just don't turn it into a funeral home, okay?"

"I got a few miles of track left on me."

They limped along through football season and into the winter.

The cops only came after hours to drink with them. One night a row of boys in blue was bellied up to the bar. Wade was behind the bar, enjoying himself as he poured, not stinting himself either. The place was noisy—cursing, laughter, animated conversation. Two cops Lemkowski and MacMillan were having a particularly heated discussion—they were both pretty drunk already—

"The freakin' Poles do all the friggin yard work and house work the Hispanics do out in L.A."

"Hey, watch it! Those are my people, man!"

Lemkowski turned away from Macmillan to Wade—

"Wade, Wade man, what is this shit? Tastes like something I'd use to clean a carburetor."

"The distributors stopped delivering the regular stuff, so I'm makin' my own. 'Downeast moonshine' I call it. Grain alcohol with fermented cider. If ya don't like that I got some home-brewed beer that Monty crafts as a hobby."

"Yeah, off-hours, when his meth lab is down."

They all laughed, the two policemen and Wade. The butt of the joke, Monty looked on sheepishly.

"How much are you in to this place for now Wade, anyway?"

"Hell, I don't know. The bills pile up, but I just toss 'em in a stack on the corner of the bar and ignore 'em, except for the gas and electric that we pay so we can stay open."

"Well, you gotta stay open. Where the hell else can we go after work? Even if I have to drink with shits like MacMillan here who insult my ancestors."

"I'm not insulting your ancestors. I'm insulting your cousins."

Lemkowski rose off his stool. He was a big man, bigger than MacMillan, but MacMillan looked like a little fighting rooster, all sharp angles.

"F@#k that, man!"

They started to shove each other, and then threw a few ineffective punches. The other cops in the bar ignored them. Then Lemkowski got MacMillan in a headlock with one arm and went for his service revolver with the other hand—

—Wade and his friends ducked down and dropped to the floor, but three other uniformed cops led by Sergeant Tomkowicz grabbed Lemkowski and wouldn't let him draw the gun.

"Hey! Hey! None of that in here. You're gonna ruin a good thing for the rest of us!" There was general muttered agreement from the other cops and Wade and his friends. "Lemkowski. MacMillan. Shake hands, and then

Lemkowski, you get the hell out of here, cool down, sober up, and don't come back tonight."

Lemkowski offered his hand to MacMillan who took it. The two men didn't look at each other.

"Yes sir. Sorry, guys." He addressed the other cops but not MacMillan, Wade, or Wade's friends.

"Don't come back here until you can maintain order."

"Yes sir, understood, Sergeant."

On the way out Lemkowski walked past MacMillan and said quietly—

"See you, you know where."

"Count on it."

Lemkowski left. The drinking went on as if nothing had happened. Where else were the off-duty cops going to go for a beer at one a.m.? The trains went by, blowing their plaintive whistles, but never stopped. Wade threw sawdust on the floor to clean up the puke. They kept drinking.

Then one night Ray came in with three other guys just like him—young, wound up and coiled tight with bad energy. Ray was lean, maybe even a little too skinny, but he had all his teeth and Monty swore he wasn't one of his meth head customers, so they didn't quite know what the hell was wrong with him. Joey, the youngest, had hard shifty brown eyes, no facial hair yet, and looked like the car thief he was. Tom was already growing fat and hair thinning even though he's only twenty-two. Jared, the college boy, with preppie looks and nicer clothes, liked to hang out with Ray and the others for the menace, the danger. Wade stopped them at the door.

"What's this?" Wade asked.

"F@#k ya, man, these are my huntin' buddies." Ray tried to shoulder past Wade, but the older man held him up with a raised hand and a grunt. They didn't touch each other.

"Gotta see some ID."

"You cardin' us, Wade?"

"Yup."

"Since the f@#king hell when?"

"Since right now, Ray. This is my place. I make the rules."

Ray glanced back over his shoulder at his three friends, all looking like they could bust up the joint any time. But Ray throttled down.

"Okay, Wade, that's cool. You got a regular gentlemen's club here, huh?"

"Ya could say that."

Ray took out his driver's license, which was expired but showed he was at least twenty-three, if you could believe it was real and not one he bought off a guy on the street somewhere. The other three handed theirs forward, and Ray took note of names without writing anything down, in case there was trouble later.

"Okay, come on in."

"Still servin' that friggin' hundred-fifty proof?"

"Yup."

"We'll take four doubles."

"They're doubles already, Ray."

"Well, make 'em double doubles then," Ray said, cracking something that wasn't a smile.

"Okay." Wade stepped back behind the bar. The other guys, Al and Jim and Jake and Monty, eased down to one end of the bar, which was nothing more than a couple door blanks on sawhorses, and talked quietly amongst themselves. Before his Marine Corps savings ran out, Wade had installed a vintage jukebox that played over tinny loudspeakers. Ray stuffed a few quarters into it and called up some death metal; fast, obnoxiously loud, dangerous. Pretty soon he and his friends were pounding along to the music on the makeshift bar, shouting their conversations, spilling their drinks, demanding more.

"Where are the cops when you need 'em?" said Jake.

Wade laughed and said: "Yeah."

Down at the other end, Joey was holding court: "You want a bike? I can get you a bike, brand new, no engine ID or a fake one. Just put in your order. Whatever you want—bigger gas tank, cushier seat, chopped, semi-chopped. I work to order." Joey was bragging, only, it ain't a brag if you can pull it off.

"Can I pay with a credit card?" Jared asked. Joey looked insulted.

'F@#k no, man," said Joey, looking insulted. "You cannot pay with a credit card. This is cash only business."

"F@#k ya can't use a f@#kin cycle in the winter," Ray jumped in. "What about cars?"

"Cars, sure, anything. The fancier the better. Beamers, Mercedes, Lexus. And snowmobiles, jet-skis, ATVs. Whatever. If it's got a big engine in it, I can get it for you," Joey boasted.

"You're a regular f@#kin' dealership," Ray said.

Tom, who had been sulking quietly, spoke up—
"That's fine for you guys. I'm not like Jared here. I don't
have that kind of money."

"The guy I know offers credit, too, but you don't want
it."

"Why not?"

"That's for suckers. The interest rate's too high, and
the penalty for not paying is—" Joey pantomimed putting
a gun to the side of his head and pulling the trigger,
jerked his head like it just exploded. It was one a.m.
already, and Al and Jim wanted to call it a night but they
didn't want to leave Wade undermanned. Monty sidled up
to Wade and whispered—"Ya want me to call Sheriff
Quinn?"

"Nah. Them boys ain't bad. They's just young. Like we
wuz once't."

"Call us if you need us. We're just up off the cliffs
there off Mountain Road.

"I know where ya live. I won't need ya."

Al and Jim went out, leaving Wade, Monty and Jake,
and Ray and his three friends filling the bar with their
explosive profane speech and the relentless music. The
two groups didn't intermingle. It went on, into a long late
night, nobody having fun, nobody willing to pack it in.
Two a.m. came and went. Wade told Ray he was closing,
and Ray said he wasn't, not tonight, they weren't finished
drinking. He'd tell Wade when he could go home. There
was a shotgun under the cash register, but everybody
knew where it was and everybody knew it wasn't loaded,
Wade's concession to the county sheriff for staying open,
so it just sat there, mute and impotent.

"Snow's starting," Jake said to nobody in particular. "I gotta get home soon or I'll never get up the damn driveway." They could all hear the poorly grouted windowpanes rattling as the wind picked up, but Ray and his buddies didn't care.

"You all should get big fo by fo's with all-wheel drive, like us. If you think you could handle 'em, F@#k ya."

This went on for another hour, to 3:00 a.m. Ray and his friends were quieter, surly, morose. They weren't good-time drunks, they were nasty drunks, all four of 'em. They threw money at Wade and spilled the drinks he brought them. Finally Wade had had enough. He motioned to Ray to join him at the one side table, if you could call it a table, it was just one of those phone company cable spools like kids used to use for furniture in college apartments, and two nondescript brown metal folding chairs.

"Okay Ray, listen, here's the deal. Jake and Monty are tired, I don't want to call the cops, so I gotta proposition for you."

"Yeah?"

"Yeah. How about I sell you the place?"

Ray registered a little surprise and sat up. "Sell The Caboose?"

"Yeah. I'm sick of it anyway. That way you and your buddies can come in here anytime and do whatever the hell you want."

"Okay. How much you want for it?"

"A dollar."

"A dollar?" Ray laughed. "You probably owe ten thousand in back mortgage and what all else I don't know."

"That's true, but I'm not going to pay it, and neither are you."

"A dollar. Okay. Here you go." Ray pulled a single from his scuffed black wallet.

"No," Wade said, "It's got to be official. I'll write up something." And he did, on the back of an unpaid utility bill, that *Wade Letourneau sells to Ray Whiting the bar known as The Caboose and all its contents for the sum of one dollar.* One of Ray's buddies and Monty witnessed it, and Wade wrote out a duplicate and they all signed that too.

"Okay, gotta go," Wade said, and he and Monty and Jake trooped out into the snowstorm, leaving Ray and his buddies to raid the scanty liquor supplies at their leisure.

The next morning there was eight inches on the ground. The lights to The Caboose were still on, and three big pickups out front, when Sheriff Quinn drove by on his morning rounds. He thought that was odd, so he pulled in and knocked on the door. No one answered. He opened it, one hand on his holster, and found Ray and three other men slumped in their chairs. He backed out slowly, reaching for his cell phone.

"Leaky wood stove flue. Carbon monoxide got 'em," the coroner explained to Sheriff Quinn an hour later as the bodies were being loaded into ambulances for the trip to the county morgue. "Ya think they'd know to check, bein' country boys. Maybe they were too drunk to notice."

"Yeah, maybe," said Sheriff Quinn.

Wade said he didn't know anything about it, and anyway, it wasn't his place anymore. He'd sold it. "Too bad about those boys. They hardly had time to enjoy their new place." Wade looked around slowly, challenging the sheriff or the coroner or anybody nearby to say something, but nobody said anything.

One Field

I love the farm fields of the Pioneer Valley, bursting with growth in mid-August. I love uncultivated clearings tucked away in forests or on remote hillsides hidden in the woods, filled with milkweed and goldenrod and common plants like clover, and edged by ancient, sacred, moss-covered stone walls built who knows when by who knows who, and left to molder in obscurity when the forest grew back in after the grazing era was over, yet so strong they remain standing, mute testaments to the character of the men who constructed them. I love all the fields.

My favorite field is an unprepossessing little field, backed up against the Pocumtuck Ridge, behind my

neighbor Dave's 1873 barn with the refurbished cupola
that's been sitting under a blue plastic tarp for ten years
waiting to be replaced on the top center of the barn. Dave
has kept the field pristine as a hay field and a private
reserve for generations of bobolinks. Once or twice a
year, at a time that protects nesting for the bobolinks, he
hays the field, using an old truck with a complicated wire
baling machine that makes old-fashioned rectangular
bales. Between the cutting of the hay and the baling
comes the *tettering*. He puts a machine known as a
tetterer that looks like a bunch of eggbeaters lined up on
a row on the back of his tractor and *tetters* the hay,
fluffing it so that it will dry in the sun.

What makes this field so special that it has won my
heart over all the other fields in the Pioneer Valley? The
bobolinks, for one thing. They are so happy here. They
are protected, taken care of, and that's the way it should
be.

But what makes this one field something magical is
what happened there one night a few years ago. Anyone
involved in farming knows that life is cyclical. One year
there'll be too much rain, the next not enough. One year
the ladybugs will overrun everything, the next year
they're absent. This one night I'm referring to, in the
middle of the summer, when the first hay of the season
was tall, Dave rang me up and said "You'd better come
over and take a look at this." Dave is a laconic fellow, tall
and soft-spoken when he talks at all. It was unusual for
him even to call me. I walked down our long driveway
and up the road to the next driveway. On the way down
our hill I noticed that it was firefly season, and there

seemed to be a lot of them. But I didn't think anything more of it until Dave met me at the corner between his house and the barn, put a finger to his lips for silence mysteriously, and gestured for me to follow him. He led me out back to the bobolink field. It was ablaze with fireflies. It glowed green and fuzzy and moving, like the green phosphorescent snow that used to appear on old-style television screens. It was a sheet of golden green, pulsing, buzzing and undulating in crazed patterns. You could stand in the middle of it, which we did, surrounded by a sea of mild, throbbing gold green fire. The fireflies took no notice of us, they were busy mating or whatever it is they were doing at this one moment in this one field. I called my wife and told her to come down, and Dave's wife Esther came out, and we stood there, the four of us, for at least an hour. It was otherworldly except that it was so much this world, so natural and wonder-ful. After, in a rare moment of spontaneous neighborliness, Dave and Esther invited us inside. Esther is as short as Dave is tall, a feisty talkative Jewish woman with curly hair and bright, inquisitive eyes. The two of them make a charmingly mismatched Mutt and Jeff couple. We talked about other amazing natural events we had seen and experienced. Dave told me about a time he'd watched a whole island rise up and float in the air in the middle of the St. Lawrence River, and he'd thought he was seeing a miracle until he realized what is was, thousands of white geese all taking off at once. I told him about the time in the Grand Canyon, sleeping in one of the side canyons on the way down to the river, when thousands of tiny but noisy frogs crossed our campsite, jumping and hopping over us as we hunkered down in our sleeping bags. The frogs were migrating to get to the side canyon's trickling stream to mate, where they made an incredible racket of frog sounds, an amphibian choral symphony. An hour later they came hopping and jumping back through the camp.

We drank cold tea and ate a pie Esther had made from berries in her back yard. We talked about fields we knew and the people who owned them or walked on them. After that night we tended to stop and talk when we passed their house and they were outside, Esther with her endless gardening, Dave working on his tractor or his truck or his boat. We became closer as couples, and we often joked that "We'll always have 'The Night of the Fireflies.'" The next year we waited for the insect explosion again, but there were many fewer fireflies that year and every year since. Perhaps it's just the cycle, or perhaps something is alarmingly wrong.

That field is more about the field than the people of the Pioneer Valley who live on it and with it and in it. That field represents the whole world for me. A world full of magic and wonder. A fragile world that could be lost so easily, if we don't make the effort to preserve it. Like the people of the Pioneer Valley, the valley itself is flint-edged, alternately warm and cold, hardy like a tenacious flower that resists all efforts to uproot it. Alternately tough and tender. Blooming, decaying, hibernating, renewing. Am I talking about the land or its people? Does it matter? One field is every field.

THE END

All photographic images taken by the author with these exceptions:

---

[i] Image from WikiCommons: https://commons.wikimedia.org/wiki/File:2_54-Band.jpg. This image was originally posted to **Flickr** by Incase. at https://www.flickr.com/photos/62021300@N00/6860044526. It was reviewed on 30 September 2012 by **FlickreviewR** and was confirmed to be licensed under the terms of the cc-by-2.0. Description: Members of 2:54, an alternative rock band from London UK, sisters Colette and Hannah Thurlow, perform at SXSW in Austin, Texas USA on March 17, 2012. These are not the women in the band in the story, but they make good visual stand-ins!

[ii] Image from WikiCommons: https://commons.wikimedia.org/wiki/File:Trase%27s_Tourist_Court,_339_Boston_Road,_The_finest_in_New_England_(83292).jpg This work is in the **public domain** in the United States because it was published in the United States between 1924 and 1977 **without a copyright notice**.

[iii] Image from Wiki Commons: https://commons.wikimedia.org/wiki/File:Trolley_trips_through_New_England_(1900)_(14592970940).jpg Original file on Flickr: https://archive.org/stream/trolleytripsthro01hart/trolleytripsthro01hart#page/n40/mode/1up

[iv] Text from: History of North Brookfield, Massachusetts. Preceded by an account of old Quabaug, Indian and

English occupation, 1647-1676; Brookfield records, 1686-1783.
https://archive.org/stream/historyofnorthbr00temp/hist oryofnorthbr00temp_djvu.txt

[v] From Digital Commonwealth
https://www.digitalcommonwealth.org/search/commo nwealth:5q47s492h No known copyright restrictions. No known restrictions on use.

[vi] Permission graciously granted by the photographer, Janet Strassman Perlmutter

[vii] Image from Wiki Commons. This image was originally posted to **Flickr** by Paul Stevenson at https://www.flickr.com/photos/53496815@N00/2822 111615. It was reviewed on 1 May 2012 by **Flickre-viewR** and was confirmed to be licensed under the terms of the cc-by-2.0.

[viii] By Dmadeo - Own work, CC BY-SA 3.0, https://commons.wikimedia.org/w/index.php?curid=2 2058976